Laurie Graham is a former *Daily Telegraph* columnist and contributing editor of *She* magazine. She is the author of several acclaimed novels, the most recent being *At Sea*. Laurie lives in Dublin. Visit her website at www.lauriegraham.com

'A joy to read. It's funny and passionate and encapsulates an era of wistful innocence.'   Maureen Lipman

'What a wonderful, life-unhancing, truly funny writer she is.'   Elizabeth Buchanan

'Laurie Graham, what a find! I was only about three sentences into *At Sea* when I knew I was going to savour every sentence and bitterly mourn the end . . . The kind of book you stay awake far later than you should do reading, only to wake bleary eyed the next day thinking of the time when you can pick it up again.'   Wendy Holden

'She has wit and insight to match Nick Hornby, and the entertainment vale of Helen Fielding, as well as depth.'   *...dent*

The Dress Circle

Laurie Graham

Quercus

First published in Great Britain in 1998 by Black Swan
This paperback edition published in 2011 by

Quercus
55 Baker Street
7th Floor, South Block
London
W1U 8EW

A CIP catalogue record for this book is available
from the British Library

ISBN 978 1 84916 397 2

10 9 8 7 6 5 4 3 2 1

Typeset by Ellipsis Digital Limited, Glasgow

Printed and bound in Great Britain by Clays Ltd, St Ives plc

For Howard

With thanks to the Beaumont Society

We was in the Tamarind Bar last night, drinking Ankle Breakers and waiting for Mary and Scouser to get back from the Jolly Roger Cruise. He said, 'Ba, we've not done bad, have we? Twenty-nine years and still going strong?'

I knew where that was leading. He's got this idea about selling up and getting a smaller place after Melody's gone. He keeps doing this. Bringing it up and then letting it rest till I've calmed down. Then he has another try. I knew he'd been thinking about it. He's been in another world ever since we got here. I said, 'Bobs, I'm not moving to no bungalow, so save your breath. Don't even think about it.'

He said, 'I wasn't.' But he don't fool me. He's thinking, if we sold Muy Linda and got some poky little place with two bathrooms, there'd be money to spend on horses. I knew this'd happen if they ever raced Nice Little Runner and he saw daylight. Three years old and all he does is eat twenty-pound notes.

First he was backward. Mack said it was because he was an April colt. Then he played up in the starting gate at Pontefract and cut himself, and then they ran him at Yarmouth and he finished after everybody had gone home. It was getting on for September then, and Mack said he'd like to try him over a mile one or a mile two. Bobs kept saying to me, 'You'll change your tune when you're in the Winners' Enclosure, rubbing shoulders with the Aga Khan,' but I've never seen the Aga Khan at Pontefract. Anyhow, little Davy Kinsella rode him for us in the Lynx Refrigeration Selling Stakes and he won by a length.

Davy said, 'He was never troubled, sir,' and I could tell Bobs liked that 'sir'. Melody was with us that afternoon. She said, 'Dad, you're not going to sell him. Not after he's won for you?' And that was that. They started the bidding and it was all over in a minute. The auctioneer said, 'Sold in' and that blummin' donkey went back home with Mack for another troughful of our hard-earned lolly. And now of course, Bobs is thinking bigger. He wants to tell Mack to look out for something in the October sales. I see him sometimes with a silly smile on his face, and I know he's just won the Derby.

I said, 'Bradshaw, you must think I was born yesterday.'

Scouser came down ahead of Mary. She was changing her shoes. He ordered two Shanghais, and when Mary saw them she said, 'Douglas! You were being poorly over the side of the boat half an hour ago.' We're all supposed to call him Douglas now, but he's been Scouser to us ever since we was in 4c and he swore the Swinging Blue Jeans' drummer was his cousin and he started talking Liverpule overnight. He didn't really change till The Move got to number two in 1967. He went back to his roots after that.

Bobs said, 'It wasn't rough, was it? We was out on our balcony and there wasn't a breath of air.'

Mary said, 'It just rolled a bit. He'd get sick on a pedalo.'

Scouser said he hadn't been sick. He said he'd been leaning over the side looking at a shark. But Mary said she hadn't seen it, and neither had anyone else.

Bobs said, 'They do get little barracudas round here sometimes, but they don't hurt.'

Makes no difference. You wouldn't get me in the sea. Why pay good money for a heated lagoon with swim-up bar and poolside snackery and then risk the sea? Anyway, Scouser said it hadn't been no barracuda, it was eight feet long if it was an inch, and it wasn't his fault if everybody'd been looking the other way.

We had Kingfish steaks and key-lime pie and then went down to watch the limbo dancing.

Bobs said, 'Why don't you ladies do a bit of shopping in the morning? Give us poor blokes time to talk shop?'

We were going to anyway. Have a massage and a wash and blowdry and then get a taxi down to the craft market. We're looking for an ornament for their new conservatory.

Mary said, 'Suits us, don't it, Ba? You can talk all the shop you like, Douglas, but don't you think for one minute we're going halves on a racehorse because we're not.'

is to have his portrait painted. There's a woman in Alvechurch who'll do it from a photo. Scouser and Mary got him Dentufix and corn plasters and a magnifying glass, and all stuff like that, for a joke.

I'd told Melody and Jason to call him, but nothing happened till bedtime, and then Jason phoned and put Roxy on to sing 'Happy Birthday dear Grandad, Happy Birthday to You.' You should have seen his face.

I had a word with Jason. I said, 'Your Dad's had a lovely day.'

He said, 'I don't know what all the bloody fuss is about. I should have thought turning fifty'd be something to keep quiet about.'

Being fifty don't bother my Bobs. He looks after himself. He goes on the treadmill every morning. He goes under the sun bed. And everybody remarks on his hair. Little Roxy always says, 'My grandad's got Sindy hair.' Not like Scouser; he's hardly got anything left on top. It's hard to remember what he looked like with hair.

Mary and Scouser never bother with breakfast, so I said I'd see her in the salon about ten. I can never do anything with my hair when we're at the seaside. Antoine suggested a turban from the cruise-wear range at Debenhams, but Bobs said, 'Strike a light, Ba, you look like Norma Desmond on a bad day,' so that went in the Oxfam bag.

There was only us two and a woman from Chicago having her nails done. Nearly the end of the season. So the girl gave us both a coconut oil treatment and that means sitting with a towel round your head for half an hour, so we thought we might as well get our nails done as well.

Mary said, 'It's not about the money, Ba. It's not that we haven't got it.'

I said, 'You don't have to convince me. I'm with

you, hundred per cent. It's money down the drain.'

She said, 'A day at the races, that's one thing. I'm not against that.'

I said, 'I agree. There's nobody likes a day at the races more than I do. Fair enough. Same as I'd enjoy going to Caesar's Palace to see Tom Jones. But I wouldn't want him on the payroll. Anyway, it's all talk. I've had this out with Bobs over and over and he knows we're not getting another horse.'

She said, 'Well, Douglas seems to think Bobs is dead set on it.'

Bobs told me it was Scouser begging him to do it, but I never told Mary that. She likes to think she wears the trousers. Fact is, we've got enough on our plate with this wedding, and the new yard opening at Rowley Regis. I know it's on his mind because he's not sleeping. Even since we've been here and he's been out on the golf course with Scouser, he's still not properly relaxed. He was up last night, out on the balcony with the Bacardi bottle, pacing up and down. Then he come back to bed, sound asleep as soon as his head hit the pillow and I lay there wide awake.

Mary said, 'I'd have to put a stop to that. It's bad enough with twin beds. At the end of a holiday that's the main thing I look forward to. Getting back to my own room. Own bed, own bathroom.'

6

Scouser and Mary have had separate rooms for a year or two now. Mary said it was because of his snoring and farting and scratching, and Scouser said it was because of her night sweats and reading till all hours. I can't imagine not sleeping with my Bobs.

I said, 'We're busy with Melody's wedding anyway. We haven't got time for buying horses.'

Mary said, 'I should have thought you'd have got an arranger to do it. You just tell them the date you want and they'll do everything for you.'

I wouldn't say this to her face, but Mary knows the thin end of beggar all about weddings. I mean, their Fleur is the same age as our Jason, and he's been married seven years and got two kiddies. Fleur's the big career woman, according to Mary, living in Seattle and supposed to be engaged, only nothing ever seems to come of it. I sometimes think Mary's a little bit jealous of me.

I had a word with Roland on the front desk about Bobs' cake. He said his Mum could have made me nice cake, full of rum and pineapple, but I wasn't know that, and at least when you buy a British as enjoyed by royalty and Hollywood stars, you what you're getting. I'd brought candles, too. sure if they'd know about cake candles in

I'd got him a half-sovereign ring, so he'd thing to open on the day, but his actual

7

We all started at Forest Road County Primary the same day. Robert Bradshaw, Douglas Vickery, and Barbara Drake. Not Mary. She didn't come on the scene till much later. But we were together all the way through. Bobs and Scouser left at Easter and went as apprentices, doing car engines, and I stayed on till July to do College of Preceptors Shorthand, Typing and Book-keeping, but I was already wearing Bobs' ring. There was never anybody else. Scouser used to try his luck sometimes, if he knew me and Bobs had had words, but I wasn't interested.

Then he turned up with Mary one Saturday night. She was the invoice typist at the garage where he worked, and she'd been at The Lady Redman Girls' School while we were all at Alfred Harris Memorial Secondary, which made her a better class of person altogether. After that, Scouser stopped mooning around after me, except when he's had a few on New Year's Eve. We've all been together ever since.

Me and Bobs got properly engaged and so did Scouser and Mary. Then we got married in the July, and they got married in the August, and we had Jason the following May and three weeks later they had Fleur. We've had some great times together, even when we were all getting started with the businesses and we didn't have a brass farthing between us. We've always had a laugh. I didn't take to Mary straight off, but she's my best friend now.

Roland done us proud with the birthday cake. He got the busboy to bring it in just as we was finishing dinner and the management threw in a bottle of bubbly. Then we went down to the piano bar and Gilbert kept the Blue Mountain Banshees coming.

Scouser said, 'Fifty, eh? Who'd have thought it? I tell you what, bloke, you don't look it. Does he Ba?'

I said, 'You haven't seen him first thing in the morning.'

Scouser said, 'All right, mate. You've got there before the rest of us, as usual. So what's it feel like? Had any twinges?'

Bobs said, 'Never felt better.' But he's a liar.

Scouser said, 'So if you could go back and do it all again, what would you do different?'

He said, 'Well, for a start-off, I'd get rid of this one. I'd get one with family money and less lip.'

Scouser said, 'Me too mate. And well-stacked too.'
Mary didn't like that.

Bobs said, 'No, I've got no complaints in that department. Seriously though, it does make you stop and think. I mean my old man never made it to sixty. And we thought he was really old, didn't we Ba? Sitting wheezing and coughing in that old cardigan. Fifty nine, and he'd never done a bloody thing. If he cleaned his pigeons out it was a bloody red letter day.'

Scouser said, 'Yeah, but you're nothing like your Dad. I remember your Dad. Always hanging about, asking your Mum for a quid till Friday. That's not you.'

He said, 'Wouldn't get me far with this one if I was. Ba's got Group 4 guarding the chequebook. All I've done for that woman and she won't even let me have a tiny little horse that'll hardly eat a morsel and make us rich and famous some day.'

When we was in bed he said, 'All them years, Ba. Our Mum was married to him all them years and he never took her on holiday once. They never went nowhere. Done nothing. It makes you think. Have you decided what colour you want for the wedding? I'll come with you. When we get back, I'll come with you. Help you choose.'

We were supposed to be going to Lindylou Bridals this afternoon to look at some more dresses, but Bobs was short-handed at the yard, so I had to go and answer the phones for him. I told Mel to go on her own. She might as well have because she don't listen to anything I say. She could have asked Kerry-Anne. She's chief bridesmaid. It's probably her job to go with the bride when she chooses her dress. Well, Kerry-Anne thinks she's chief bridesmaid, and she should be by rights because she's been our Melody's best friend ever since I can remember. But there's been a bit of manoeuvring by the Godbolds. Andrew's got a sister and Mrs Godbold has let it be known she thinks Jennifer should be the main bridesmaid. I think Kerry-Anne and Jennifer should just share it. Nobody's going to be looking at them anyway. If anybody's going to steal the show it'll be little Roxy.

Anyway, I phoned Mel at the boutique. I said, 'Your dad needs me down the yard, so we'll have to do Lindylou's another day.' Then she started.

She said, 'We've got to. It's by appointment only. You can't just turn up another day.'

I said, 'So make another appointment. It's simple enough, Melody,' but she was in a right old state.

She said, 'This is all I need. How am I ever going to get this wedding organized if people keep letting me down? And I've had a letter from the vicar, saying he hasn't seen us in church, cheeky bastard. I've told Andrew to send him a fax. Tell him we might take our business elsewhere. And now we're not even going to look for my dress. It's not fair. I'm going to phone Dad. He can manage without you.'

I got to him first though. I said, 'Don't you dare. She's got to realize. If there's no business, there's no money for wedding dresses.'

He said, 'Take her. We'll manage here. I don't like to see her disappointed.'

But I said, 'No. I'm on my way. And I want you hundred per cent behind me. I'm warning you.'

He said, 'I shall have to go. She's on the other line.'

Bobs is down in London at the Motor Trade Show, He wants to go computerized for wheel alignment and body jigging. He said, 'I'll stop over. Have two days there, and look at the engine steam-cleaners as well.' He wants to get the Rowley Regis side of things really set up for Jason, real state of the ark. And he is right. That's what you do for your kiddies. He always says, 'We can't take it with us, Ba. And I'd sooner spend it on them now and give them a start in life than have them scrapping over it when we're gone.' I hate it when he stops over, though. I never sleep properly when he's not there. Don't sleep properly when he is there neither, not these days. And then, when I do manage to nod off, I wake up in a sweat over the wedding. I've no sooner knocked one thing off the list and there's half a dozen more I hadn't even thought about.

We have got the dress. We'd narrowed it down to a beaded corset bodice and full skirt, but there was a gold and ivory one with a tulle skirt, and there was one with a dark-blue satin piping detail and big puffed sleeves, and there was a jacquard halter-neck, which was my favourite. She was in and out of the changing rooms, trying them all on, over and over, and then she burst into tears and said she needed her dad. She was hysterical. Mrs Butler that runs Lindylou's was very nice. She made us a pot of tea while I got Bobs on the mobile, and he come straight over. He told her she looked like a princess in all of them, but he did lean towards the ivory and gold, so that's what she had, with a flyaway veil, gold and pearl circlet and over-the-elbow gloves.

Then he dropped a bombshell. He says to Mrs Butler, 'While I'm here, I'm thinking of a Nehru jacket for myself. Have you got anything?' First I'd heard of it. Andrew's having morning dress. His best man's having morning dress. And I've told Jason he's got to wear morning dress. I said, 'You can't go messing up the arrangements now. It's already settled.' But he said, 'We don't all have to match. If the Godbolds jumped in the canal, would you? I think it'd be nice to go for something a bit different,' and Mrs Butler fetched him one in bottle-green velvet, and one in terracotta silk, with a little leaf design on it, and a toning waistcoat.

He said, 'What do you think, Mel? Nice white collarless shirt under it? Get my streaks done?'

She seemed happy about it. That's the way it goes with Melody. Daddy can't put a foot wrong, and I can't do anything right. But at least we've got her dress. There's still trouble with the vicar, which the Godbolds seem to be blaming entirely on Mel.

Bobs said, 'Cancel it. We'll have it somewhere else. It don't even have to be a church. Not any more. We could have it at home, like they do in Hollywood. Or we could have the whole thing at the golf club. I'll have a word with the steward. We've got the room booked for the do afterwards, so it'd be easy enough for them to get married there too. Might be nice. I mean, St Leonard's; it's not anything special, is it? It's a gloomy looking joint. How come we're not having it in a cathedral? We've got enough people coming.'

It's for family reasons. Andrew's Mum and Dad were married at St Leonard's and they wanted to carry on the tradition. And, of course, there's no sign of their Jennifer getting wed. There won't be, neither, from what I've seen of her. If she was mine I'd have to get that chin fixed. They can do it now. Shave a bit off the bone. Two weeks in bandages and she'd be a different girl.

Anyway, there's all this stuff to do: bridesmaids' dresses, flowers, cake, music, invitations, personalized serviettes, buttonholes, cars, store lists, hair, shoes, photos, video, and Bobs keeps disappearing. He's been up twice to Mack's to watch that donkey on the gallops, and now he's stopping in London, two nights. One night would have been bad enough. Two nights, and when I phoned the hotel last night he was out. It was nearly midnight before he phoned me back. Said he'd been for a balti with somebody called Harry he'd bumped into at the show. He said, 'You remember Harry. Used to have a panel-beating business in Bromsgrove?'

I've been thinking back, but I can't remember him, and neither could Mary. She said, 'I'll ask Douglas. Perhaps he's not been at the show at all. Perhaps he's got a woman down there. How did he sound? I can always tell if Douglas is lying to me.' Which just goes to show how wrong Mary can be.

Nice Little Runner's got laminitis again. Mack's got him on antihistamines and cold-water footbaths. It don't sound good to me. He's off his food, but the vet's bills'll be making up for that. Bobs come off the phone with a face like a damp dishcloth. He said, 'Mack thinks we should be prepared for the worst.' I thought he meant shoot him. Then I felt bad. But Bobs said, 'No, you fool. Lay him off for the summer. Maybe try him over hurdles once his feet are right. He might make a chaser.'

He's going down there on Sunday with a bag of Mintoes and a get well card. I said, 'You can't afford to be daft about him. He's only a horse. We can't keep him in a nursing home.'

He said, 'I shall do the right thing. Come with me. It'll be a nice drive out.'

But I can't because Jason's bringing Diane and the

kiddies over so we can go through Melody's wedding magazines and decide on bridesmaids' dresses.

I said, 'You'll miss Roxy and Blair. Go another day. Horses don't know any different.' But he wouldn't be budged. He went off to play with his putting machine and I hardly had another word out of him all night.

We'd had a nice day though. We got a train to London early. Bobs had got to see somebody about this steam-cleaner they're getting, and then he met me at Knightsbridge tube. We had pan-seared scallops on a confit or something, and Bobs asked for vinegar, and then we had an afternoon round the shops, getting me my rig for the wedding.

I've got a Parma-violet silk dress and jacket with lovely little covered buttons running up from the cuff, and a cream picture hat with ostrich feathers with the tips dyed gentian blue. Bobs picked it all out. It's better than going with Mary any day.

He said, 'Now for your flowers, Ba, you want something bright yellow,' and the woman in Harvey Nichols said, 'Exactly. Just what I'd have suggested.' Bobs was quite taken with a red two-piece as well, and a cream foulard jacket with a new-length skirt. He was up and down the rails, holding things up for me. But it was no contest really.

The woman said, 'Will you be accessorizing today?'

Bobs said, 'You're not expecting me to buy new shoes for her as well, are you? Spend, spend, spend. She can wear her jogging pumps and be grateful.' I don't think she realized he was joking.

We had a nice wander round afterwards. I got a squeaky rabbit for Blair and Bobs got a thing for Roxy, like squishy plastic in a little tub, and when you move it about it sounds as if somebody's blowing off. He wanted to take me for tea at the Waldorf, but I wanted to get back. London does me in. He's up and down there all the time, specially lately, and he comes back full of beans, but I feel sorry for people that have to live there. I look out of my lounge window and there's nothing but lawns between me and the golf course. We get foxes coming up, and badgers. We even get little bambis in the cold weather. Anyway, he don't need to take me to the Waldorf. Thirteen pounds for a few cakes and sandwiches. I know we can afford to do it, and I know my old man'd be willing to do it. And that's good enough for me.

Roxy said, 'Where's my grandad?'

I said, 'He's had to go and see that poorly horse,' and then I got the crayons out for her while we made a start on the magazines. Kerry-Anne had brought some from the salon, too. Andrew was supposed to be dropping Jennifer off at eleven, but we started without her.

It was going to be bad enough getting Mel and Kerry-Anne to agree on anything, without a Godbold clouding the issue. Last thing Bobs said to me on his way out was, 'Remember, democracy don't work. Specially not with bridesmaids.' I don't think Melody had got anything like that in mind anyway.

Jason cleared off. I said, 'Drive down to Mack's and keep your dad company,' but he didn't fancy it. Diane wanted him to take Blair for a bit, like the dads do these days, but he didn't fancy that neither. Then, just as he was leaving, Andrew pulled up with Jennifer, so the pair of them went up to the clubhouse for a drink. Jennifer said, 'Isn't this exciting! I've never been a bridesmaid before.'

I thought, No. And you wouldn't be being one this time if it wasn't your brother's wedding. We're going to have to keep her in the background for the photos. It's funny. Andrew's not a bad-looking boy. The chin seems to come from his mother's side, and he's got more of a look of his dad. And he's definitely got brains because you have to go to college to be a lawyer. All these years I've walked past their offices on Park Hill and heard people talk about them, Godbold, Ives and Liquorish, and I never dreamed our Mel would end up marrying one of them. Course, Andrew's not a full partner yet, so the Godbold on the brass plate is his father.

They had us round for sherry when Melody and Andrew got engaged. Draughty old place with no carpets. Just little bits of rug, and the arms of the chairs all threadbare. We couldn't believe it. All that money lawyers make. You'd think they'd get themselves a bit of carpet. For Melody and Andrew's wedding present we've said we'll do their kitchen for them. Cooker, fridge, washer-drier.

I said to Melody, 'What are the Godbolds giving you?' and she says, 'Andy's being made a partner.'

Which is very nice, but you can't hardly put a ribbon round it, can you? I mean, it'll be nice for the future, but it's not like buying them their bedroom suite. Bobs don't really agree. He says it's security for them. He says it could come in handy having a brief in the family. Handy Andy, he calls him, since Mel told us. I suppose they'll have to get a new brass plate for Park Hill, because after the wedding it'll be Godbold, Ives, Liquorish and Godbold.

Roxy's got her heart set on pink, but I know Melody's not keen. She's been looking at red or green or dark blue. I said, 'Mel, red's meant for winter weddings. And you've got be careful what colour you put Roxy in: she looks like a little candle as it is.' Then Kerry-Anne had a brainwave. She said, 'Me and Jennifer could have one colour and Roxy could have something else. Like she could have peach, and we could have cream trimmed with peach. I've seen it done. And we could have bouquets, and Roxy could have a Victorian hoop decorated with flowers. I've seen that done as well.' And so that's what's been decided, I think. They're all going out next Saturday to try and get something and Diane's going with them to be referee.

Roxy fell asleep on the floor. She done a picture of a horse with a nurse and then flaked out, and Blair got hold of her crayons and scribbled on the wall a bit. Diane went spare, but it'll wash off. I only buy washable.

I said, 'Did she have a late night?' but Diane says she's been drooping around all week. There's probably something going round at school. We left her for a bit and then the phone woke her. She was in a right old monkey mood. I done her jumbo sausage and twister fries, which is her favourite. Bobs always pretends to nick her chips and makes her squeal, but she didn't even want that.

Melody said, 'You'd better buck up if you're going to be my bridesmaid, Roxanne. You're going to have to stand still and hold your hoop nicely.' She's never had any patience with kiddies, our Mel.

Scouser come round in the afternoon. I don't know what he thought he was doing coming then. He knew Melody'd be at work, and Bobs has said, it's her choice. She can have whatever she wants. Scouser said, 'Tell her she can have a Silver Spirit Rolls, but not the Silver Cloud because that's already booked. You always have to book early for a Silver Cloud. Or there's the Bentley, which'd be my favourite, or the white Daimler, or a nice old Armstrong Siddeley.'

I heard Melody saying to Kerry-Anne on Sunday how she fancied a four-in-hand with liveried coachmen, but I didn't tell Scouser that. He might have gone off in a huff, or more likely he'd have said he could get a carriage for her, no problem, and then we'd be on tenterhooks, wondering if he was going to come clean and admit he couldn't do it, or turn up with an old rag-and-bone cart and swear it was from the Royal Mews.

He said, 'Or I've got a 1926 Model T, but if she's wearing a long train I wouldn't recommend that. Or, now this might be the go, we've got the stretch Cadillac. And that *is* a lovely motor. That really does turn heads,'

I said, 'You'll have to leave her the brochure, Scouser. I can't tell you what she wants. You should have come on a night-time, or the weekend. There's no sense in coming round when I'm on my own.'

He said, 'That's just where you're wrong, Ba. I can't think of anything nicer than dropping in here of an afternoon. Is the kettle on?'

I said, 'What's the matter? Have they forgotten how to make tea at your place?'

He said, 'So where was the old man off to in such a hurry?'

I didn't know what he was talking about.

He said, 'Just now. Headed for the motorway.'

I said, 'My husband don't have to clock in with me every hour. He's got businesses to run. Have you cleared it with Mary about coming round here?'

He said, 'All right, all right. And I don't have to clock in with Mary. I do as I please. Any biscuits?'

I said, 'Have you heard the latest? About the horse?'

'*Heard* the latest?' he said. 'I am the latest. I signed

the cheque. And like Bobs told you, not a word to Mary, It's a surprise for her birthday.' I had to stop and think for a minute how I was going to handle that one. He didn't notice. Scouser never notices anything.

I gave him a tea bag in a mug and a couple of digestives. I said, 'Well it's a big thing, getting involved with horses. They never get little problems, horses. They only get big ones. And then they start costing.'

He said, 'I know that. I've gone into it with my eyes open. And Mary'll love it. And I hope you don't mind about the arrangements. Any time one of them is running, you and Mary can take turns who'll go up for the trophy if it wins. Bobs drives a hard bargain, but I had to insist on that. Halves on everything. That's the only way to do it.'

I don't know if it's Bobs who's so clever or Scouser who's so thick. And with anybody else it could be the end of a beautiful friendship, but not with Scouser. He's wanted a horse ever since we got one. And now he's got a half-share of this joke with the bad feet, and he's putting money in the pot for Mack to go shopping at the sales, and he thinks he's Donald Trump.

I said, 'Have you talked to Mack?' Of course he hadn't talked to Mack.

He said, 'As you know, Ba, Nice Little Runner is

very highly strung, specially when they're getting him ready for a race . . .'

Specially when they're getting him ready for the cat-meat factory.

He said, 'I'm not telling Mary till we get to the course. I'm just going to make out it's an ordinary day at the races, to see him run and give Bobs a bit of support like, and then I'll give her the Owners and Trainers badge, just before we go into the paddock. And I'll get your Jason or somebody to video the look on her face. It'll be a picture. She don't know a thing about it. Not a thing.'

I said, 'Your secret's safe with me.' It is until Bobs gets home tonight. After that it might be a front-page murder story.

He said, 'So you don't know where he was off to in such a hurry?'

I said, 'Any news from your Fleur?'

'No,' he said, 'I don't believe there is. You're a handsome woman, Ba. You're better looking now than when you were fifteen, and you were a belter then.'

I hate it when he starts up. Specially when all he's had is tea.

He said, 'Things might have been very different. If Bradshaw hadn't staked his claim, you might have been Mrs Vickery. Still could be. You've only got to say the word.'

He's round the bend.

He said, 'Yeah, it was probably that blonde he was with. Young bit of stuff. Is it her that answers the phones?'

Scouser knows very well that Pam answers the phones and she's got glasses and a boy in the Army. He's never seen Bobs going anywhere with a young blonde. He's such a stirrer.

I said, 'No, it'd be Michelle Pfeiffer. No, I'm wrong. It's Thursday. It'd be Claudia Schiffer.'

He said, 'I mean it, Ba. Say the word and I'm yours.'

There's quite a lot of things my friend Mary don't know about her husband.

Melody wants a Silver Cloud or an open landau; Bobs thinks they should scrub the church, have the whole thing at the golf club, and hire a helicopter; and the Godbolds sent a message with Mel to say we're welcome to use their Rover. I said to her, 'What do they mean? Use their Rover? Do they think we can't afford a proper wedding car? We could use our Merc, as it happens, but we're not going to. Don't tell your dad what they said.'

But of course she did. She's got a mouth like the Channel tunnel. I thought he'd hit the roof.

'Well,' he said, 'I suppose they're only trying to help.'

He was in front of the telly then all night, watching Sky Sports. I couldn't settle to anything. I said I was going to do half an hour in the gym, but I didn't do much. I sat on that exercise bike arguing with myself, and then I did something terrible. I went through his pockets. I kept thinking I could hear him on the stairs. I kept running to the door to check. I couldn't even be sure which blazer he'd been wearing. He always hangs everything up as soon as he's taken it off. He's always took care of his clothes. And there was nothing in any of his blazer pockets because he don't leave things in his pockets. So I had to go looking for his wallet. And I knew there wouldn't be anything in it. Only his cards, and photos of me and the kiddies, and a few receipts. I was that mad at myself, letting Scouser wind me up.

I said to him later, when we were in bed, 'Scouser said he seen you. When he was on his way here with the brochure. He said you didn't notice him.'

He said, 'About three? Yeah, we were going to pick up a panel job from Kidderminster. I had young Gary with me. I tell you, that kid, he never stops eating. Crisps, Curly-Wurlies, bananas. He got in the truck with all his grub like we were driving to the North Pole. And he's not got an ounce of fat on him.'

I said, 'Do I know Gary?'

He said, 'You've seen him. He's not been with us

long, but you must have seen him. Fair hair. Ponytail and an earring. What are you smiling about?'

I had to tell him something. I said, 'Just something Scouser said.'

'Oh, yeah . . .' he said, 'I was going to tell you. Obviously. Only he hasn't told Mary yet, so I thought . . . I didn't pressure him, Ba. He's been wanting a slice of the action ever since we got Nice Little Runner. And if he don't look into things properly, it's up to him. He could have phoned Mack. Anyway, he knows there's been a few problems. He's happy. He's happy, I'm happy, Mary'll be bloody delirious. How about you? Are you happy?'

I said, 'And what about going in with him to get another horse? I thought we'd had all that out? I thought we'd agreed.'

He said, 'Well, it's not definite. Maybe we will, maybe we won't. Don't worry about it. You know I don't spend money I haven't got. And nothing's definite.'

Scouser thinks it's very definite. He can see Mary collecting a silver salver from the chairman of Ladbroke's and getting her picture in the papers.

Bobs said, 'Anyway, sometimes it's nice to have a secret on the go. Some things are best kept quiet until you're sure about them, I only didn't tell you because

Mary don't know. So what else did Vickery have to say for himself?'

I said, 'Not a lot. Still wants to know when I'm going to marry him.'

He said, 'That's one of the things I like about Scouser. He doesn't know when he's beaten.'

I said, 'This wedding's putting years on me. It's a good job there's no more after Melody.'

He said, 'Did you though? Did you ever think of choosing him instead of me?'

There's never been anybody for me but my Bobs. He knows that.

I said, 'Still do. Don't you underestimate Scouser. He could do things for me you couldn't.'

He said, 'I know. Give you a free ride in a pink Cadillac. That's what worries me. You're doing a great job on the wedding though, Ba. You're a star. I was thinking, when everything's sorted, you ought to have a couple of days at Wernley Spa. You know? Have a massage. Get your nails done. Then you'd come back nice and fresh for the wedding. I was talking to a bloke at the club. You'd know him. Big red-faced bloke, got a roofing business out Droitwich way? He was saying how his wife got quite poorly worrying about their girl's wedding, and then she had a weekend away and come back a new woman.'

I might do. That's one thing about Bobs. He does think of me. I wonder when he's going to give me whatever it was he paid thirty-nine ninety-nine for at Sasha Lingerie on 5th April?

We've had the luxury cake bags printed with *Melody and Andrew* and the helium balloons as well. The Godbolds have squared things with the vicar, so that's a relief. I'd have had to get 200 invitations printed again if they hadn't sorted him out, although we're not home and dry yet because they've had a few words over the music. Melody wanted 'Whiter Shade of Pale' and 'Love is in the Air' but the vicar said it'd have to be something more traditional. I don't see why. We're paying. And they can't have bells because they've got falling masonry.

Bobs said, 'Sounds as if this padre needs to get his act together. It's not too late to change your mind, princess. You can still have it up the golf club and be legal.'

I said, 'Don't tell her that. I want this settled, once

and for all. She can have hymns like everybody else. It won't hurt her.'

We met Scouser and Mary for a drink and a bit of dinner. They'd heard there was a new landlord at the Hare and Hounds with a little Chinese wife who does food. They've certainly spent some money on the place. You used to be able to write your name in the nicotine on the walls. But they've knocked a wall down where the snug used to be, and had a big new window put in. Grey carpet. Pink serviettes. Don't look like a pub at all any more.

Bobs said, 'Guess who we towed in today? Guess who had our number in her car on account of our policy of lady driver priority that was dreamed up by my clever wife here?'

Mary said, 'Show business or royalty?'

Scouser said, 'Royalty don't call out breakdown trucks, woman. They make their own arrangements. It won't be anybody. You see. It'll be somebody who was in *Crossroads*.'

Bobs said, 'Well that's just where you're wrong, my son. It was Kimberley Kendrick off *Midlands This Morning* and she'd had an argument with a milk tanker.'

We'd ordered Thai Green Curry and Singapore Noodles and it came in the tiddliest bowls, like a starter, not a dinner. Bobs looked at the woman and then he looked at the food. He said, 'Is there a war still on?' She didn't catch on. I can't see her doing much good trying to run a pub.

Scouser said, 'Look at that pair over there. That pair of queers.' So then Mary kept turning round and saying, 'Where? What, them? How can you tell?'

Bobs said, 'What is your problem, Vickery? They're just sitting there, eating their rations same as we are.'

Scouser said, 'You've changed your tune.'

But he hasn't. Queers have never bothered Bobs. Interfering with kiddies, yes, but poofters, no.

Mary said, 'I wouldn't mind them if they stayed at home.'

Bobs said, 'Well, if I felt like arguing with you, I'd say it has to take some guts to be like they are and not try to hide it. I'd say they've got balls and they're not bothering me. Only I'm not getting into an argument with you about it because you've had two gin and limes so you'll only talk a load of twaddle. Did Ba tell you, she's having four days at Wernley Spa? They do a pre-wedding special for the bride and her mother.'

Scouser said, 'Yeah. Not long till the big day, is it? Mary could come with you.'

I said, 'I think they're booked up for the dates we're going. You should have said sooner. Anyway, you'll be able to treat her when Fleur comes home and names the day.'

She said, 'Fleur's busy with her career. That's the trend these days. It's only the ones that haven't got a career that go in for big fussy weddings.'

Melody's not having a big fussy wedding. She's having Handel's Lager and biodegradable confetti.

Scouser said, 'Of course, we get more contact with celebrities in our line of business. We had Gene Pitney, remember? We had his road manager enquiring about the presidential stretch.'

I said, 'He never hired it though, did he?'

He said, 'We had Jan Leeming when she opened that garden centre.'

Me and Bobs stopped for a kebab on the way home we were that hungry. He said, 'Do you fancy getting in the back for a cuddle?'

I said, 'Not with my back I don't.'

He said, 'I've just thought, Ba. What music they should have at the wedding. They should have "Unchained Melody".'

The bridesmaids are having peach organza with corset lacing and flower circlets in their hair. Diane phoned up. She said, 'I'm getting Jason to bring Roxy's dress round to your place for safe keeping. She's everlasting wanting to try it on while it's hanging up here. And what's happening about the hen night? I mean, I don't mind arranging something, but it's Kerry-Anne's job really. Or Jennifer's.'

I said, 'You can forget that. Jennifer won't know about hen nights and Kerry-Anne couldn't organize a smell in a gasworks.'

Diane said we could have a four-course dinner, with topless waiters, disco and one free drink for thirty pounds a head at Big Nite Out. I said, 'Sounds all right to me. Talk to Melody. I've got enough to think about. I've got Bobs' sister and her husband arriving and the Godbolds coming for drinks and little nibbly things. Do whatever you think, only keep Mel off the Southern Comfort, and do it early in the week. Give yourselves time to recuperate. We don't want all of you looking like dogs on the wedding video.'

Jason come round about seven.

He's a good boy, really, and touch wood there hasn't been any big bust-ups since they've been in business together. I never thought it'd work out. Bobs has always been so hard on him. Course, when he was a baby, Bobs was working all hours getting the first yard going. He used to come home fit to drop. We hadn't got family we could borrow from. Every month it was the same thing. Pay the bank, and then do the best we could with what was left. Many a time we were on bread and soup by the end of the month, and he's a big man, my Bobs. Scouser and Mary were in the same boat. I think that's why we've stuck together through the years. They had two rooms at her mum and dad's house when they were starting out, so there'd be money for the business. They were there until Fleur was three or four, sharing the kitchen and the bathroom and everything. I used to meet Mary. We used to put Jason and Fleur in their pushchairs and push them round for hours, didn't matter what the weather was like, just to get out of the house. We used to say Fleur and Jason might end up getting married, the Bradshaw empire and the

Vickery empire, but once they'd got to about nine they couldn't stand the sights of one another. I've thought sometimes that Scouser would never have gone into business if we hadn't. He's always copied Bobs, and Mary can be a very envious woman. They've done well, though, I will say that. We all have. Considering how old Hubble used to throw the black-board duster at us and tell us we were all a waste of space and we'd end up on the shoelace counter in Woolworth's, we've all done brilliant. And Jason wasn't much of a scholar neither. But we never let him think he was set up for life with a nice successful business. Bobs always said to him, 'Get your exams. We could do with somebody in this family that can handle the VAT.' And he did. He wasn't interested in the cars the way Bobs was. Him and Scouser had always got an engine in pieces years ago. They got sump oil on Mary's lovely white towels one Sunday and I thought Scouser's hide was going to end up a hearth rug. Jason was always more interested in the business side of things. He looks nice in a suit. And he married Diane and now he's a family man. They haven't had things as hard as we did, but people don't these days. Everybody starts off with a tumble-dryer. Bobs said, 'We can help them so we will help them, Ba. Just because my dad was a miserable old git don't mean we have to make a tradition of it.' And Diane's a lovely girl. I couldn't ask for a nicer daughter-in-law. She keeps the house nice, and the kiddies. I think it's having the kiddies that's brought Bobs and Jason closer together. I mean, the day Roxy was born you'd have thought Bobs had won the pools. He was down that hospital with a six-foot teddy and she was only a few hours old. In fact, he held her before Jason did because Jason was frightened he'd break her. We hardly slept that night, we were that excited. He lay there saying, 'We shall have to get a net put over the pond, Ba. Perhaps we should get it filled in. We shall have to get her a swing. And a little playhouse. We can get her a pony.' Melody's always been his princess, but the last six years Roxy's been his real number one.

Melody was out at her Cordon Bleu class. Jason stopped for a Scotch and they started watching the boxing. I was going to hang Roxy's dress in my wardrobe, but then I thought it'd be better somewhere where I'm not in and out all the time and it wouldn't get squashed. So I took it down to Bobs' boy's room. He's got his pool table in there and his computer for some day when he's going to write the story of his life, and there's a bed-settee for if ever we've got a full house, and a nice big cupboard with hanging space and drawers at the bottom.

There was some old junk in there. A dinner suit I thought had gone to the Cancer shop, and a waxed jacket that needed a new zip. And a red crystal pleat two-piece, size 18, that wasn't mine and wasn't Melody's, and didn't have any reason to be hanging in a cupboard in my house that I could think of, except bad, horrible reasons to do with blondes seen riding in cars and receipts from Sasha Lingerie for thirty-nine pounds ninety-nine.

I kept busy in the kitchen till Jason had gone. I got all the bottles and jars out and gave the shelves a good scrub. He come in, looking for cheese and crackers. He said, 'Uh-oh. Spring-cleaning at nine o'clock at night. Something's up. What have I done?'

It was him should have been trembling, not me. Banging around, looking for pickled onions. He said, 'It's only the Godbolds coming. And my sister. You're not going to have Health and Safety inspecting your cupboards.'

He knew. He kept his back to me, but I could tell he knew.

I thought of saying, What about your cupboards? Have you got anything in them you wouldn't want inspected? I thought of saying, What's her name? only I didn't want to know. I didn't want to know anything

45

about her. I just wondered who else knew. Scouser? Mary?

We just stood there. In the end I said, 'I've put Roxy's dress in the closet in your boy's room, so it don't get squashed. It'd be a pity if it got squashed.'

He said, 'Yeah.'

Then he said 'I've been wanting to talk to you, Ba. I've been meaning to get round to it, only it never seems like the right time.'

That wasn't what he was supposed to say.

He said, 'There's not a man alive got a better wife than I have. I've always told you so.'

He has.

He said, 'I've tried to find a way round it. I really have. But there isn't a way round it. I was going to talk to you when we were on holiday, but that didn't seem right. And then I thought I'd wait till after the wedding. See, there's always something.'

I said, 'Who knows?'

He said, 'Nobody. Well . . . Nobody.'

I said, 'So that means half the golf club knows. Have you taken her there? Where have you taken her? Who's seen her? Am I a complete blummin' laughing stock?'

He said, 'No. That's not it at all. There isn't nobody, Ba. I swear to God. It's me. It's my stuff. I've got shoes and undies and everything. You're the best wife in the world. I just like dressing up. It don't mean there's anything wrong with you. If there's anything wrong with anybody, it's me. Only I don't do anybody any harm. A lot of men do it, Ba. You might not realize it, but a lot of men do it. It's only like . . . like an interest.'

An *interest*. He's got a red crystal pleat two-piece in his cupboard, and things I haven't even seen that he wants to wear. I've known him since the day we started school. We've got grandchildren, and a daughter who's marrying a solicitor, and he's trying to make out it's an *interest*.

Cactuses are an interest. Or badminton.

I said, 'Have you seen a doctor?'

He said, 'It's not like that.'

I said, 'No, you're right. It's nothing like that. You've been caught buying your fancy woman presents, and all you can do is try to wriggle out of it, pretending to be a pervert. I've heard of some stunts in my time, but this one beats them all.' I said, 'Why can't you just own up? Be a man? Let's get it over and done with.'

He said, 'That's about the size of it, isn't it? You'd be happier about it if I'd got another woman. You'd sooner be married to a cheating bastard than some-body who just wants to wear a frock every now and then and not do nobody no harm. Eh? Is that it?'

47

I don't know. How should I know? We were all right till Jason brought that bridesmaid's dress round. We were happy as Larry. He says he was just waiting till after the wedding before he told me, but he wasn't. He knew I don't want to hear stuff like that.

He said, 'I'll sleep in Jason's old room tonight.'

He said, 'You think something like this'll fade away as you get older. You think you'll stop wanting to do it, but you don't. And then fifty comes. You get to fifty and you think, if there's something you want to do, you'd better get on and do it.'

He said, 'I love you, Ba. If I could have carried on without you having to know I would have done.'

He didn't though, did he?

I hardly slept a wink, but I must have drifted off for an hour because when I come down at seven he'd gone. I had a cup of tea in the kitchen and then I went to have a look in that cupboard to see if he'd got rid of it. If he'd got rid of it I was prepared to say no more about it. But there it was. So I took our Roxy's dress out of there for a start off. I wasn't leaving her lovely bridesmaid's outfit hanging in the same place as that horrible thing.

When the paper came I made some more tea and went back to bed. Terrible things in the paper. A man gone haywire with a gun in New Zealand, and another kiddie missing, just nipped out to the chip shop and not been seen since, and some church doing lesbian weddings. There's something going wrong in the world today. And what I want to know is, if he's got shoes and undies, like he says, where's he got them hidden? And where's he been wearing them? I mean, he's six foot three. He's got a big nose. He stands out a mile anyway, without dressing up like Dame Edna.

Melody come in with her face all blotchy. I hope they can do something with her at Wernley Spa. She said, 'Dad's gone early. I've got to talk to him. He's got to have a word with Andrew.'

I said, 'Now what?'

She said, 'My honeymoon. It's all messed up.'

It was supposed to be a secret. Andrew said he'd arrange something and it could all be a big surprise for her when they left the reception, which was a very nice romantic idea. That boy does surprise me sometimes. I did say, though, she'd have to have some idea so as to know what to pack. I told her to find out if it was going to be beach or smart. She said, 'Course it's going to be beach.' And I did say, 'Well check anyway. He might be taking you to Paris.'

She said, 'He knew I wanted to go to Bali. He knew that's where I thought we were going.'

I said, 'So where are you going?'

She said, 'Scotland. He's booked some stupid cottage on the Isle of Skye. He's so mean. He's so tight. Dad's got to talk to him. He said, "You told me you'd like to go to an island." He's so stupid. I've bought my bikinis. And I can't get a refund on them because I've taken the panty-protector strip off them. I told him, "If it's the money, my dad'll pay." But he said, "The money's not the point, Melody. The point is for us to have a romantic fortnight without running up a big Visa bill." He said we can go for long walks. This is his mother. They're always going hiking and staying in little cottages. I said to him, "I'm not cooking on my honeymoon." Dad's got to talk to him. Tell him it's not on.'

I said, 'Your honeymoon's nothing to do with your dad. Anyway, he's busy today.'

She said, 'We could still book for Bali.'

I said, 'You might be able to book, but you haven't got time to have all your jabs.'

She said, 'What?'

I said, 'Typhoid, cholera, hepatitis. Anyway, you don't have to cook. You can eat out.' Course, then she just stuck her fingers in her ears like she used to when she was little and we told her it was bedtime.

She said, 'I don't want to hear about any of that.'

I'm going to get four days of this at Wernley Spa. I'm going to be sitting around all day long with a crowd of women who've got normal husbands, and I'm going to be cooped up every night with Melody, going on and on about Andrew says the Godbolds don't do things this way and the Godbolds don't do things that way. Three hundred pounds a night and I'm going to come home wrecked.

I said, 'Melody, stop your whining, sort your honeymoon out with Andrew, and stop picking your toenails on my duvet.'

'God,' she said, 'you're a moody cow. I don't know how Dad puts up with you sometimes.'

I said, 'Much more of this and I'm cancelling the health farm.'

She said, 'Yeah, you do that. Everybody else is trying to ruin my happiness, so you might as well join in. You know your trouble, don't you? You want to get yourself some hormones.'

I threw my hairbrush at her but she got out of the door too fast.

The doorbell went about eleven. It was a little man hid behind a big bunch of flowers. Carnations, Love-in-the-Mist, all sorts, all wrapped in cellophane with a ribbon and a card. *Sorry*. That was all it said.

He phoned in the afternoon. He said, 'Am I allowed home tonight?'

I said, 'Can't stop you, can I?'

He said, 'You know what I mean. We shall have to talk about it, Ba. Sooner or later.'

So I said, 'Well, let it be later then. I don't want to hear a word about it until after the wedding. Not a word. And you can get rid of that . . . thing . . .

hanging in the closet. I've got people ringing up about the gift list, I've got the caterers wanting numbers, and the way Melody's shaping up we could have the whole thing cancelled at the last minute anyway. I've got seating plans to do.' I said, 'It's bad enough, the way them Godbolds have been looking down their noses at us. If anything like this come out, we'd be finished in Bromsgrove, Bobs. A thing like that, the word'd soon get round.'

He said, 'So I can come home then?'

I said, 'You'll have to. Don't you dare not. Else that'll be round like wildfire.'

He said, 'I do love you, Ba.'

I said, 'And if Melody collars you about her honeymoon, you're not to get involved. I've had her screaming at me first thing because she's just found out they're going to Scotland.'

He said, 'Scotland can be very nice.'

I said, 'Not when you've bought a tie-dye sarong,'

He said, 'She already phoned me, anyway. I told her we had a week in a caravan at Weston and we thought we were millionaires.'

I don't know about millionaires. I had cystitis, and if I could have found a vet I'd have paid him to put me down.

Mary phoned. She said, 'Guess what? Douglas has got me into Farthing Hill Hydro for the weekend.

Three hundred and fifty pounds a night for an en-suite in the Premiere Annexe and priority service in the treatment rooms. I'm getting my allergies tested and a skin peel.'

I said I'd drive. I thought it'd keep my mind off other things. We had a stack of magazines in the back, and wine-in-a-box, and Mel had got Maltesers and Doritos, in case she couldn't handle it. I said, 'I don't want to hear about weddings, honeymoons, Godbolds, bridesmaids, nor nothing. I'm having every treatment they've got and I'm going home looking ten years younger, so I don't want you doing anything to put years on me. Understand?'

She said, 'There'll be people my own age. I shan't be hanging around with you,' and as it turned out there was a little group of youngsters in, but they were princesses from Kuwait or somewhere and I don't think they knew the lingo.

You have to have a session with one of the staff after you've checked in, so they can design your personal health and beauty programme. I said to her,

'You needn't bother weighing me because I'm happy as I am.' I told her I wanted scrubbing and oiling and massaging. I told her I wanted three square meals a day and something to get rid of the pain in my neck. She said, 'I'll book you in with Madame Lin for a Thai massage on Sunday.' She couldn't have been more than eighteen herself.

Anyway, Saturday morning I pretended to be asleep till Mel had cleared off for a jog. That girl's never jogged in her life and she never will again if I know anything. She's not built for it. Hundred pounds for a pair of trainers and they won't see the light of day again. I had a late breakfast and a lovely facial with Julie, and then I wandered out in my robe and got myself a reclining chair by the dipping pool. I could hear them in the proper pool, through the terrace doors, doing aquarobics.

I got talking to two sisters from Swindon. Wendy and Paula. They weighed twenty-six stone between them and Paula said they were supposed to get five pounds off, each, in ten days, but Wendy said, 'I've got yo-yo weight gain. My doctor told me. But I'm not here to be miserable. I have enough of that at home.' She'd got a husband who wouldn't let her learn to drive, and one daughter who keeps washing her hands over and over, and another one who's been done for shoplifting and had her name in the paper.

She said, 'What are you here for then? You're not fat.' So I told them about the wedding. They thought that was really lovely. They thought I was dead lucky. Paula said, 'We never had children. My husband said it was probably him because he did have the mumps when he was a lad, but it didn't take his girlfriend long to get pregnant. He's fifty and she's twenty-three, and now they've got a little baby boy.'

Wendy said, 'He sees her all right for money though. Don't he, Paula? She says she'd sooner have had a little baby, but they only grow up and break your heart. And at least he always let her have her own cheque-book. That's more than I've ever had. I mean, I can have anything I want. Trevor's not mean. I only have to ask. But it's not the same as having your own chequebook.'

I said, 'Well how does that work? Say you see a pair of shoes?'

She said, 'I tell him how much they are and he gives me the cash. He says if I had a chequebook I'd only get in a mess with it. Are you coming to line up?' It was ten to twelve and they wanted to be at the front of the queue when they opened the doors for lunch. I said I'd probably see them later.

Mel come searching for me to see if I thought she looked any thinner yet. She said, 'They had somebody famous here last week. I can't remember her name, but she was in films years ago with a big bosom. They were talking about her in the sauna. She's been married four times. And you see that woman with her hair in a red scrunchy? Her husband's a top doctor, and he hits her, but only in places where it won't show.'

Men are horrible. Even the ones that don't hit you or stop you having a chequebook. They're always belching and scratching themselves and giving people the finger just because they got into a parking space first. They can't behave nicely like we do. Not for more than five minutes at a time, anyway. Our Jason's no better. Blowing off on purpose in the lounge instead of holding it in till he gets outside. He wasn't brought up to behave like that. And Melody wouldn't dream of doing such a thing. Men are just horrible. Even the nice ones.

I bet there's nobody else here though that's had a terrible shock like I've had. A terrible shock that you can't tell anybody about as long as you live. I've gone over it and gone over it, and I still can't think what brought it on. We've always been good pals. Always pootled along. Never had any problems in the bedroom department. He says he's always been like that, but I don't see how he could have been. I mean, why would he have got married and settled down if he knowed he was abnormal. There was a story in one of Mel's magazines about a man who left his wife and kiddies to move in with another man. Said he'd been living a lie. But Bobs swears there isn't anybody else. He swore it on his grandad's New Testament he had with him all through the First World War, so I do believe that. But the other thing is, how would somebody like Bobs know about stuff like that? He's never bought mucky mags. And where we grew up there wasn't any weird stuff going on. You got married, had your family and that was that. And if you didn't get married it was because you had to stay home and look after your old mum, or you were one of them confirmed bachelors, like Larry Grayson, or maybe you were so ugly nobody'd have you. But there was never any men turning into women or lesbians having babies or anything like that. And drugs. People go on about the swinging Sixties and how everybody smoked LSE, but we never even seen any. Lem-Sip is all I ever took. Still is.

I had a go in the jazzercise class, but I was creased after ten minutes, so I went for a walk in the grounds till it was time for my pedicure. I seen Paula. She said, 'Come to our room tonight. We're having a party. We've got wine and Malibu and crisps. Bring whatever you've got. We're going to stop up late and have a real laugh.'

I'd told him I wouldn't be phoning home. He said, 'Quite right. You need a proper break. And if the world ends I expect you'll hear about it.'

I said, 'My world's already ended.' That gave him something to think about while he's there on his own. It was good timing, really, me and Mel coming away this weekend. Give him a taste of being all on his own and make him realize what he'd be giving up if he carried on with that nonsense.

I did just check at the front desk, but the girl said, 'No, sorry, Mrs Bradshaw. Still no messages.'

I was going to get an early night, but Wendy come hammering on the door about nine o'clock. Mel was having a go at music therapy. They all lie round on mats and listen to classical. Wendy said, 'Come on. You're not sitting in here all on your own. Everybody's down in our room and that Shirley's been down to the little shop in the village and bought up all their chocolate-chip slices.'

They were smoking themselves silly. You'd have thought they'd just got off a desert island. Anyway, I thought I'd have a drink with them. I weren't really tired and there was nothing worth watching on the telly. They were larking about though, doing the cancan, singing 'My Way'. I weren't in the mood for anything like that.

I got talking to this woman called Margaret. Lovely speaking voice. You could tell she didn't really fit in.

I couldn't see her doing the conga. She said, 'It's like being back at school, isn't it? Seeing how much you can get away with before Matron catches you?'

I said, 'I used to read about them kind of schools in Enid Blyton. The school I went to, we didn't have a matron. We had a headmaster that used to play pocket billiards and the nit nurse once a term. I always fancied it though, boarding school. Anything to get away from the heap we lived in. I wouldn't have got homesick.'

She said, 'You would have if you'd had to spend Christmas there, just you and a house mistress.'

Her people had been in Africa, growing coffee. Just like that film with Robert Redford.

I said, 'Llandudno was about as far as we ever got. We've made up for it since. We always go somewhere nice for our holidays. And we have thought of Africa. One of them safaris where they drive you round and you see the lions.'

She's been married nearly thirty years as well, although he's quite a bit older than her. They've got two boys, grown up and doing well; not married or anything, but got good jobs. And she's having a little break because they've had his mother living with them until her Alzheimer's got too bad, and they've just moved house, and it was all getting on top of her.

She said, 'I feel a bit of a fraud being here, really.

I'm not dieting and I'm not that bothered about having slices of cucumber put over my eyes. I can do that at home. I think maybe I should just have gone off somewhere. Gone on a painting holiday. Or India. There are so many unhappy women here.'

I'd only had a couple of drinks. It's not like me to start crying in front of strangers. I don't think anybody else noticed.

Margaret said, 'Why don't you get some sleep? Or do you want to talk?' She said, 'I'm not leaving till lunchtime tomorrow, if you want someone to talk to. Sometimes sleep's the best thing, though.'

I didn't know what to do. It would have been nice to tell somebody, specially if I was never going to see them again. But you never know. If you tell someone a secret and then they don't say what you wanted them to say, that makes it worse.

I said, 'I'm not sure.'

And she said, 'When in doubt, don't.' You could tell she'd had a proper education.

Melody was watching *All-Night Shopping* when I got back to the room. She said, 'Where have you been? Where's our box of wine? You look awful. You want to get some reflexology. It's lovely. They do it on your feet.'

She turned the sound right down, but the flickering from the screen was still bothering me. Then I was just floating off and she said, 'I phoned Andrew. He's bought little silver boxes for Kerry-Anne and Jennifer, one of those bunny rabbits dressed like a bride for Roxy, and a shaving brush with a silver handle for Tim.' Tim's his best man.

She said, 'And I phoned Dad. He's all right.'

I said, 'Any messages?'

She said, 'Not really. He was having steak and kidney pie out of a tin. And they're going down to Mack's tomorrow. Him and Uncle Scouser. Mack's got a horse they might buy.'

If it's true, what he says, then anything else could be true. He could be a murderer. He could have a boyfriend set up somewhere. We've never had secrets. But if he's telling the truth now, that means he's had a big secret all the time I've known him. And there's no reason he wouldn't be telling the truth now. Nobody'd make something like that up. Unless he's telling one fib to cover over another fib, which brings me back to, is there another woman? But if there is, it don't make any sense covering it up with a nasty story like that. I mean, lots of husbands have another woman. Probably most of them. Like Scouser. He would if I just said the word. So, if Bobs had, I wouldn't be very happy about it, but it'd be better than knowing he was turning into a woman. It'll be in the papers, and the kids'll have to know. He'll have to go far away. Start a new life. The businesses'll be down the toilet. Fifty years old and I shall be living in a caravan.

He could see a doctor. They can do things with electric shocks. It might take a while, but we could maybe get him back to normal before anybody hears about it . . . Keeping the lid on it, that's the worst. If I don't tell somebody I shall bust, but it isn't the kind of thing you tell people. It goes away for a few minutes, and then I remember. And I've got to go home to it. I've got wedding presents arriving, got to be checked off on Melody's list, and the cake and the florist to check up on, and people staying over, and the rehearsal. I haven't got time to get into another big row about this. I've just got to keep quiet and be nice to him, and hope to God he don't do anything silly. He might even have got over it. Now he's come out with it and told me, and he's had a few days without me, had time to think, that might have got it out of his system. And Mel'll be gone, so we'll be able to sit down, no interruptions, and just lay it all to rest. Start afresh.

Madame Lin made me lie on a little mat on the floor. She's only tiny, but she hasn't half got some strength. She was pulling on my toes and fingers till the joints cracked, which sounds horrible but it did feel quite nice. But then she started on my neck and shoulders. I thought she was going to kill me. I thought I'd be leaving in an ambulance. I've never heard snapping and squelching like it. I was laughing, only it wasn't funny. I mean, you pay good money in a place like Wernley Spa, and you don't bother asking to see their certificates. I was scared stiff, only I couldn't stop laughing. She said, 'Is good. Is good,' and then she pulled my arms round, like a strait-jacket, till I couldn't laugh and I couldn't even breathe. I just lay back down on the mat, and she covered me with a duvet and said, 'Is finished. You rest.' And I was glad she'd closed the blinds and left me to it because I cried and cried and I don't even know what for.

They bring you a cup of tea after a while. You can have ordinary tea or herbal. You just tell them when you book the massage. The girl said, 'Are you all right, Mrs Bradshaw?' They're all so young.

I said, 'I don't know. I feel very peculiar.'

She said, 'Everybody does after Madame Lin. A lot of people ask to have their dinner on a tray in their room afterwards.'

I asked her to cancel my manicure and find out if that Margaret had left yet, but she'd checked out hours since, and they won't give you addresses or phone numbers. You've got to respect people's privacy.

Mel said, 'I've lost two pounds. Do I look thinner? And I've had an eyeliner lesson. That other girl who's getting married is having a pearl choker. Do you think I should have a pearl choker?'

I told her I didn't really care.

She said, 'You are such a cow sometimes. It's my big day and you're not even interested. You're never interested in anything that's going on in my life. It would have served you right if I'd just run off and got married in some grubby registry office. You'd probably have liked that. Some people's mothers are grateful to have a wedding to look forward to, but I have to have a family that couldn't care less. I'm your only daughter. This is going to be your only chance to do the right thing. You weren't like this for Jason. You've always made more of him. You've never been interested in me.'

After I'd smacked her she said, 'You want to get yourself some HGV. You want to stop making everybody's life a misery. I tell you what, I feel really sorry for my dad, what he has to put up with.' So I smacked her again.

Pat and Gus were supposed to be coming down Thursday for the wedding on Saturday, but now all of a sudden they're arriving Monday. Anything for a free holiday. Pat's his sister, so we had to invite her. We never see her from one year's end to the next because she lives in Dundee, but you can't have a big wedding and not invite family.

She's younger than Bobs, and then there was another sister, Jean, but she got polio and died. We get a card from them at Christmas and that's about all. The dog signs it as well. They put its paw on an ink pad and it signs all their cards. I suppose it's because they never had children.

I said to Bobs, 'I hope you made it clear the dog's not invited?' He said, 'No. Yeah. They won't bring a dog all that way. What could you do with a dog on the motorway if it needed to go?' You can never trust men with arrangements.

So I've put them in the twin beds with the view of my pergola with the clematis. And that means they'll have the blue bathroom to themselves and they won't be getting under our feet on Saturday morning. Kerry-Anne's sleeping over on Friday night, and Jennifer. Not Roxy though. Diane thinks she'd get overexcited, so Jason's going to drop her off first thing with her hair in curlers, and then they'll only have Blair to see to.

I had Roxy yesterday, while they were getting their carpets cleaned. She was as good as gold, playing at weddings with her Sindys. I done her turkey melts and baked beans for her tea, but she hardly touched it. I hope she's not going down with something. She said, 'Nana Ba, will you be coming to my wedding?' I said, 'Course I will. Who are you going to marry?' She says, 'My grandad,' and Melody said, 'Roxanne, don't be silly. I hope you're not going to act silly when you're my bridesmaid.'

Mary was round to tell me about the hydro and bring the extra bedding we're borrowing. She said, 'There's a car just pulled in. Bloody cheek. There's people just pulled into your driveway and now they're giving their dogs a bowl of water.'

Pat said, 'Haven't we made good time? I bet you

didn't think we'd be here yet. We're all right though. Don't bother about us. We made a thermos and we stopped for our sandwiches at Lancaster.'

Gus come in, struggling with a pair of boxers. He said, 'Tyson, Bruno, meet your Aunty Barbara,' and Mary said, 'No, I'm Mary. I'm married to Douglas.'

Pat said, 'You chump, Gus. *This* is Ba. It just goes to show how long it is since we've seen any of you. And didn't you used to be married to Scouser, Mary?'

Apparently they got Bruno to keep Tyson company. Apparently he got very destructive because he was bored and lonely.

Gus said the best thing would be if he gave the dogs a guided tour, so they felt more at home. He said, 'You haven't got any cats, I hope?' He said Tyson kills cats.

Pat said she hoped I hadn't gone to a lot of trouble because they'd brought everything with them. Bedding. And a little portable TV to keep them company if they had to be left on their own. And food. She said they'd be all right with tins just for the one night, and she'd boil up some lights and ox liver for them in the morning. She said, 'And just wait till Melody sees what we've got for them to wear on Saturday. Special wedding collars with little bells on.'

Gus was outside with them, kicking their doggy-do into my rose bed, and Mary was whispering really loud all the way to the door. She said, 'I wouldn't have them in the house. Tell them they'll have to stop out in the car.'

I said, 'What? Till Sunday?'

She said, 'Well, it's up to you, but I would. Get Bobs home. He should tell her. She's his sister. And your lawn'll be ruined. You'll have yellow patches everywhere. And the other thing is, Ba, when you write the little cards for the table, the little place-cards for the reception, I hope you'll remember it's *Douglas*.'

I phoned Bobs. He said, 'I'm on my way.'

We've been all right since I got back from Wernley Spa. We've been that busy we haven't had time for any trouble. Least said, soonest mended.

He come in and he shouted, 'Ba, there's a pair of porkers running round your patio. Didn't you tell the butcher you wanted them slaughtered before he delivered them?'

Pat said, 'Still trying to be a comedian, then?' And Gus said, 'Good to see you, Bobbie. And don't you worry about our wee laddies. They'll be no bother. We take them everywhere, don't we, Pat? They're grand company. You'll hardly know they're here.'

Bobs said, 'As long as they're not chewers, that's the main thing. And as long as they haven't got fleas.'

Pat said, '*Fleas?* Bruno's sire was Charlemagne

Roisterer of Montrose, and one of Tyson's sisters got Best of Breed at the Grampian Show last year. Our dogs don't get fleas.'

Bobs said, 'Right. So even if they did, they'd be a good class of flea. Fair enough. It's just that, when you've got kiddies scrubbing round on your carpets, you don't want them taking any little visitors home with them. Because Blair, that's Jason's youngest, he's just starting crawling. So we have to be careful.'

Pat said, 'There's nothing wrong with our dogs,' and Bobs followed me out to the kitchen, pretending to fetch ice cubes.

I said, 'Well, you handled that one firmly.'

He said, 'It's only for a week. And they'll be all right. At least they haven't got long hair shedding all over the place. They do look clean, you must admit.'

I said, 'And what if they snap?'

He said, 'They don't look nasty. They look half asleep.'

I said, 'They've had tranks to keep them quiet for the journey. It'll be a different story in the morning. And they'll have to take them out somewhere to do their business. We've got the Godbolds tomorrow night and I don't want the garden full of blowflies.'

Pat helped me clear away later. She said, 'You don't need to do a big dinner for us every night, Ba. We're not big eaters. And don't worry about the boys. As long as you don't make any sudden movements near them they're like little lambs.'

When Melody told us she was seeing Andrew Godbold from Godbold, Ives and Liquorish I was really pleased, because some of the lads she used to bring home were more interested in her car than anything else, and most of them hadn't got two halfpennies to rub together. Not that money's everything. There was one time when Bobs really lost his rag with her and that don't happen very often. It was over a boy off a council estate in Rubery, and he hadn't got a proper job because he was in a band. Mind you, they were only seventeen. Bobs used to say, 'He'll never amount to nothing.'

It was a five-minute wonder, anyway. She packed him in when he forgot Valentine's Day. I did say to Bobs though, 'Well, I married a lad off a council estate, and I done all right.' He said, 'Yes. But Melody has had an education.'

We've spent some dough on them kids. They both went to Silver Birches till they were twelve. Then we tried Jason at Massingham, but he hated the boarding so we brought him home and got him into Cockfield as a day boy. Bobs said we should make him stick it out, but I talked him round. Melody boarded at Gayton Park, just Monday to Friday, and she loved it. All the different outfits they had to have. One kind of blouse for netball and a another kind for lacrosse. One August Bank Holiday I sewed in 120 name-tapes.

Melody was never very sporty because of her puppy fat, but she made plenty of friends there, like Kerry-Anne. She got her GCSEs in Domestic Science and Social Studies, and then we sent her to La Fontaine to be finished. It was only in Kent, but she picked up more French in six months there than she ever did at school because they used to go on day trips, and she learned all about who sits where if you've got say a duke and a lordship coming for their dinner the same night. So she's going to be a real asset to Andrew. It's just a pity about his family.

Even Bobs was nervous and he don't care what anybody thinks about him. I'd told him he'd have to get Pat and Gus to go out. We'd got Moët in the fridge, Chardonnay, beer, and that elderflower stuff in case Audrey Godbold wasn't drinking, and then we'd got Scotch, gin, Remy Martin, port, and three kinds of sherry. I kept putting nuts in little dishes, and as fast as I was putting them out, he was eating them. He said, 'Have we got enough mixers? Should I get Armagnac? What about olives?' We don't even like olives.

Then Pat come in with her coat on. She said, 'Now are you sure?' She said they'd been wanting to see *One Hundred and One Dalmatians* but it was hard to get baby-sitters at home, so if we were sure . . .

I said, 'Where are they?'

She said, 'They're tucked in upstairs, and they're watching *Wish You Were Here*. We've explained to them where we're going, and they seem all right. If you could remember to pop up at half-past eight and switch over to *Brookside* for them. And these are their chocolate buttons, just in case they get upset.'

They'd been gone about five minutes when the howling started, like an air-raid siren. Then I heard the Godbolds' car doors. I said to Bobs, 'I shall never forgive you for this,' and just as the bell went at the front they stopped howling and started barking, and he said, 'Cinzano, Ba. We haven't got Cinzano. I'll be five minutes.' Five minutes. We're not five minutes from anywhere.

You'd think a solicitor's wife would keep herself looking smart. She must have to go to functions. Not that I was dolled up. I just had a nice little suit on, palazzo pants and a big loose shirt over a little silk vest; just a nice bit of evening cruisewear. But Audrey. It looked to me like something home-made. It looked to me like she'd run it up from a remnant and it had had a hard life ever since. I hope she's got something better than that lined up for Saturday. I can see why their Jennifer's such a sad case.

Bobs was gone half an hour, and they don't drink Cinzano anyway. She had a sherry and he had a whisky, and by the time he got back them dogs were bouncing off the walls upstairs. You could hear them scratching my lovely new paintwork, but I didn't dare go up and open the door. I was never so glad to see that man in my life.

He said, 'Why don't you show John and Audrey round the garden while I go and throw another gladiator in with the lions?' They laughed.

He was shaking when he caught up with us. He said, 'Well, I've separated them. I think that's the best I can do till Pat gets back. I've put one of them down in my snooker room.'

John Godbold said, 'How did you get it to obey you?'

Bobs said, 'I didn't. It wriggled past me before I could get the door shut, so I just followed it downstairs and shut it in the first room it went in.'

I said, 'Did you put the telly on for it?' He said he

hadn't thought of anything like that, and there wasn't much left of the pillows in Pat and Gus's bedroom. Then Audrey said she had a knack with dogs, so her and Bobs braved it and went and put a *Pot Black* video on for the one that had escaped, and chucked the chocolate buttons in for good measure. So that left me with John.

He's nice enough. Nice manners, but a bit shy. My Bobs can talk to anybody.

He said, 'Well, not long till the big day. We just hope they're prepared to put the work in. They've had every advantage in life, Andrew and Melody. But people give up too easily nowadays. One tiff and we get them in our office, asking about a divorce. We had a couple, not long ago, arguing over who should pay for the wedding photographs. Straight back from their honeymoon and in to see a solicitor. But we know Andrew and Melody have got more sense than that. I'm sure they know they have to settle down and work hard at it, after all the big fuss. That's the advice we've given them. Expect the worst and hope for the best. We've had cross words over the years. Who hasn't? But we never let the sun set on our wrath. And Melody's got a good example to follow as well. There aren't many young people these days who still have parents living at the same address. We're an endangered species, Barbara.'

Bobs and Audrey were the best of friends when they come back from sorting the dogs. Like old buddies back from the war. We went back in the house because there was a nip in the air. John and Bobs got talking about who used to own what house, because that's the side of things Andrew and his dad are involved in, and who'd got the receivers in, because Bobs always likes a bit of gossip, and I showed Audrey my albums of Roxy and Blair, and then the old ones of Mel and Jason when they were kiddies. Then Bobs cracked open the Moët and we were well away. Audrey said 'My word, *champagne*,' as if they never drink it in their house. We had them little smoked-salmon things from Marks', and dips; and I was just thinking how it had gone a million times better than I'd ever dreamed, when one of the dogs come tearing in, wild-eyed, with slobber all over its jowls and something in its mouth. I couldn't work it out for a minute.

Audrey said, 'My word, that's a big shoe.' And it was. When you see a size 10 in a man's shoe it don't look anything out of the ordinary, but when you see a size 10 black-patent stiletto, that does make you sit up.

I thought he was going to hit it. I've never seen Bobs look so mad. But he just pulled and pulled to get it out of its mouth, till the shoe come apart, and there he stood with the heel in his hand, and the dog made off with the rest of it hanging out of its mouth, dragging itself along by its front legs, scraping its bottom all over our sculptured Wilton.

Audrey said, 'I think that young man needs a worm powder.' I put my glass down, and I never touched another drop.

He said, 'I know what you're going to say.' Which was a funny thing, because I didn't. All I could think was I'd got to get through the wedding. Get through Pat and Gus being here, and the house being full of people coming and going, and having to look nice for the photos and keep smiling. Come Sunday afternoon it'll be just the two of us.

We used to talk about that. All the things we'd do when the kids were grown up and gone. He used to say, 'Every weekend we should do something special. Even if it's only going down the garden centre and spending a few quid.' We always looked forward to being on our own again. We've always got on. And now he's gone and ruined everything.

I couldn't even bear to look at him. I was clearing away after John and Audrey left, and he kept following me around, getting under my feet. He said, 'Nobody thought anything of it, Ba. It was just a shoe. They thought it was one of yours.'

They did not. Size 10.

I said, 'You promised you'd get rid of it all.'

He said, 'No I never.'

That was what was so hard. If he'd been a-begging me to forgive him, or even if he'd just said he was sorry, it wouldn't have been quite so bad. We all back-slide. I used to be forever starting diets and then buying them big bars of Fruit & Nut. But he didn't even look upset, except over the shoe being ruined. He was carrying on like *I* was being unreasonable.

I said, 'Don't you dare do anything else to ruin this wedding.'

He said, 'Is that what you think? When have I ever done anything to hurt my family?'

It's true. He never has. Not till now. He's always been a diamond. But that don't make this business right.

I said, 'Don't you start twisting things. You know what I mean. How am I supposed to get through this wedding with a smile on my face when my husband's turning into a woman and he won't even go to the doctor's? When you haven't even tried to get any tablets for it. I don't think you've even tried to sort it out.'

He said, 'I am not turning into a woman.'

I said, 'We'll have to put a good face on it till Pat's

gone. After that you can move your stuff into Melody's room. I don't want you anywhere near me.'

He said, 'There aren't any tablets for it, Ba.'

Then Pat and Gus got back from the pictures and that blummin' dog was finishing off the shoe just inside the kitchen door, happy as Larry, wagging its stump. I heard her say, 'Tyson! Have you been playing up for your Aunty Barbara?'

I said, 'Well, here's something you can sort out. Tell her there's a door needs repainting and I'm not having her dogs in the same house as my grandchildren.'

I went up to bed. Didn't even say good night to them. She'll owe Mary two new pillows as well. He come up not long after. I'd heard them talking downstairs, and there were no raised voices so you can bet your bottom dollar he never told her any of the things I said he had to tell her. Anything for a quiet life. That's him. Thank the Lord that dog never got in where Mel's dress is hanging.

I was just clinging onto the edge of the mattress so I wouldn't touch him, with my shoulder all scrunched up under me.

He said, 'I'm sorry the way it turned out tonight.'

I never answered him, but he carried on anyway.

He said, 'I want this wedding to go off all right just as much as you do. I promise you, I'm not going to do anything to spoil the wedding. And then, after it's over, I want us to talk about, you know, and I want to put your mind at rest. I want us to stay together, Ba. Because I love you, and we're a great team.'

He was crying.

I said, 'There's no need for that.'

I gave his hand a bit of a squeeze. That's what we always do to start making up.

I said, 'I just want everything to be all right for Saturday. After all that work.'

He said, 'I know. And it will, I promise. Great team, eh?'

And I did feel a bit better after that. I'll bet there are some tablets you can get. There's tablets for most things these days.

We was both up before seven. I had another look at
my lists and Bobs made tea. I took a tray in to Kerry-
Anne about eight and she was wide awake already,
but we left Mel till later. We weren't due at the hairdresser's till eleven. She was still sound asleep when
I went in, thumb in her mouth.

I said, 'Your Dad's cooking you your favourite.'
She said she couldn't face breakfast, but then in he
come wearing his bra and suspenders barbecue apron,
so she perked up. He'd been out the back and picked
a rose for her, and he'd done her orange juice, French
toast and maple syrup.

Gus was out early to give them hounds a good long
run. He'd been taking them out every five minutes
since the incident the other night. Not that we've had
an apology. All Pat said was 'we shouldn't have left
them. We never leave them. They must have thought

we were never coming back.'

And they went out and bought two pillows but they weren't as good as the ones that got shredded. Everything's always got to be done on the cheap with Pat. She's the exact opposite to Bobs. You'd never think they were brother and sister. And we never see them. Only weddings and funerals.

I had my bath so we could put the flowers in there, as soon as they were delivered, and shut the door to keep them safe. Then when we looked properly we realized they'd delivered the Godbolds' carnations to us as well, so Bobs had to go chasing down the drive after the van.

He said, 'I thought we agreed we didn't want carnations? I thought we'd agreed on rosebuds for all the men and a camellia for Audrey?'

We did. They must have gone in and changed it. They're old-fashioned, John and Audrey. They probably thought rosebuds for men was a bit way out.

He said, 'Should I come with you to the hairdresser's? Get your boy to do me a quick wash and blow-dry?'

I said, 'You can't do that. You haven't got an appointment.' He should have made an appointment. They'd got me to do, Melody, Kerry-Anne, Roxy, Diane, and Jennifer Godbold, and God knows they'd got their work cut out with that one.

He said, 'I heard you ask Pat if she wanted them to try and fit her in at the last minute.'

I said, 'I only asked because I knew she'd say no.' Pat won't spend out on hairdressers. She does it herself with Amami setting lotion. And Bobs has always made his own arrangements. He's been going to Lorraine's in Kingsbridge Street for years. He used to have perms there, when perms were in. And now she does his highlights. He invented unisex in Bromsgrove, my Bobs.

His hair didn't need doing anyway. I said, 'If you want to make yourself useful, get round to the golf club and make sure they've remembered the balloons.' Then Diane arrived. She'd got Blair on her hip, grizzling with his teeth. Jason was supposed to be having him so Diane could concentrate on Roxy, only he'd suddenly decided he'd got to go to the timber yard. His sister's wedding day and all he could think about was shelves.

Bobs said, 'I'll take the nipper with me. If I take Diane's car, with the baby seat, he can come and watch me blowing up balloons. He'll be all right.' So then Roxy started up. 'I don't want to have my hair pulled tight. I want to go with my grandad.'

She cried herself into such a paddy, Diane couldn't do nothing with her. And Melody kept saying, 'You're not being my bridesmaid if you've got puffy eyes, Roxanne,' till I could have strangled her.

Bobs was the only one she'd listen to. He said, 'You haven't got time for sitting in the car getting bored. That's what babies do. You've got to get done up like a fairy princess. And your Nana Ba's got a secret to tell you,' and he was miming behind her back for me to take her out in the garden and tell her about the new horse.

She calmed down a bit once we were outside, but she wouldn't leave go of me. Her little arms were clamped round my neck like her life depended on it. I could see Melody giving me the evil eye out of the kitchen window and pointing to her watch, making out we were going to be late.

I said, 'Grandad's getting something you don't know about, and after Aunty Melody's wedding, one of the weekends, we're all going to go for a drive to see it. So what do you think it is?'

She said, 'Is it new teeth?' That's because Scouser sometimes takes his dentures out to make her laugh and she's always on at Bobs to get teeth you can take out.

I said, 'No. It's something that's got four legs and it eats Polo mints.' So then she guessed. She wanted to know its name. I said, 'Perhaps Grandad and Uncle Scouser'll let you help them choose a name.' If it was left to me it'd be called Money to Burn. If it was left to me it'd be called One Born Every Minute.

She said, 'Nana, I don't feel very well,' and it is true, she does look a poor pale little droopy drawers. I mentioned it to Bobs later on. I said, 'Do you think I should say something to Diane?' But he said, 'She's all right. It's just the excitement.' But I don't think it is.

Mel did look lovely. They all did really, even Jennifer after the hairdresser had done with her and Kerry-Anne did her eyes. And Bobs looked the business in his Nehru jacket. When I seen him bringing her down the aisle, I thought, 'Well, I backed a winner with this one.' Specially when I looked across at Scouser with the light bouncing off the top of his head. Mary's told me she thinks their Fleur'll have a quiet wedding over in America and just phone them up afterwards to tell them. She says she's not bothered, but I think she must be. They've never had the kind of luck we've had. Scouser's always laughing and joking, but things haven't worked out as well for them as they have for us. Even if we have had a little bit of bother recently.

When the vicar said, 'Who gives this woman?' Mel had to give him a nudge. We'd been through it all at the rehearsal, but he don't pay attention. We've never been churchgoers. You could see Andrew's side knew all the words to the hymns without reading the brochure, and we just had to keep up as best we could.

He whispers to me, 'When do we have to kneel down?' Well, it was his idea of a whisper. I said, 'We don't. It's Church of England. When he says, "Let us pray", just hunch over and close your eyes.'

When we come out from signing the register they played that lovely wedding march. John Godbold said it was from *Midsummer Night's Dream*, but that's Shakespeare and I'm sure he never wrote any tunes. John's been to college, though, so he ought to know. Anyway, we had to lead off behind Kerry-Anne and the best man, and Bobs and Audrey come after us, and I could see everybody in the audience laughing at something, well, everybody on our side. So I turned round, and it was just Bobs, making a meal of parading out, doing his Prince Charles impersonation, nodding and waving like royalty.

That church weren't what I'd have chosen. It was a gloomy hole. But when we got outside it was blazing sunshine. It couldn't have been nicer for the photos. Pat fetched the dogs from the car and put frilly wedding collars on them. And there were some lovely outfits. Lots of pastels and lovely hats, and Bobs weren't the only bloke who'd gone for a silk jacket instead of a morning suit, specially the younger crowd. Some of them I didn't recognize straight off because I'd only ever seen them in T-shirts and jeans. Gus was in his kilt, of course, so that was a conversation piece. Some of Andrew's side were a bit shabby. Some of his aunties, I suppose they were. I mean, it was probably good stuff in its day, but you could see it was years old. You'd think they'd splash out a bit for a wedding. I wonder sometimes what these people do with their money. Bobs reckons they've all had shrouds made with inside pockets.

So we all piled up to the golf club, and they weren't properly ready for us. There was supposed to be trays of sherry, and when we arrived there was just a little waitress running round looking for glasses. She said, 'The dishwasher's just on rinse and dry.' I said to her, 'Don't you put our sherry in hot glasses, young lady. My husband's been a member of this club for fifteen years.' And Audrey Godbold kept trying to smooth things over. She said, 'Well it gives us all time to powder our noses.' None of her business.

Melody was in a mood with Andrew because he wasn't wearing the cufflinks she'd bought him, and she was in a mood with Kerry-Anne because she'd got her the wrong colour tights, and she was in a mood with me because she's always in a blummin' mood with me. Then Roxy was trying to ask her something. I could hear her little voice, 'Aunty Melody, Aunty Melody . . .' and Mel said 'Oh for goodness sake, Roxanne, pipe down. You're always wanting something.' Which wasn't true. She'd been as good as gold in church, and remembered where to stand, which is more than could be said for some people. We hadn't had a peep out of her.

Anyway, Bobs stepped in. He said, 'I dunno Rox. Your Aunty Mel's only been married half an hour and she's turned into an old grump already.' He said, 'Let's go and find you some lemonade.'

I had to sit between Andrew and his dad at the top table, and then the question was, whether Kerry-Anne was going to get the end seat, being as she was supposed to be chief bridesmaid, or Jennifer, being as she was family. Me and Mel never had sorted it out. But then Jennifer said she could sit next to her dad any day and she was quite happy to go and sit with Jason and Diane and Roxy. That was a nice thing to do. They are nice people, these Godbolds. Just a bit behind the times, that's all.

It didn't really strike me till we were sitting down to the seafood panache, I can't have said more than a dozen words to Andrew in all the time I've known him, and now he's as good as family.

He said, 'What am I going to call you now?'

I said, 'What do you think?'

He said, 'Well, I asked Melody's dad, and he said he'd be happy with *sir*.'

We decided on Ba. I told him about our wedding reception. A sandwich buffet at the The Lord Kelvin and my dad picking a fight with everybody because he'd been on the rum since opening time.

He said, 'I really admire people who make something of themselves when they haven't had every advantage, you know? I really admire people who build up a business from nothing and stand on their own two feet.'

I don't think he'll be seeing a lot of that from Melody.

He said, 'I was a great admirer of Margaret Thatcher. Still am. I wish we could have her back. She knew what people could do if they worked hard and didn't sit around feeling sorry for themselves.'

I said, 'Well, if ever you drop by the yard, you'll see Bobs has got a signed photo of her. He met her. She come to Birmingham and he met her. You ask him. He loved that woman.'

So that got us off to a good start with the new son-in-law. The rack of lamb was nice, but the veggies was lukewarm when we got them, so they must have been stone-cold by the time they served them down the bottom. I'd told Bobs to write down what he was supposed to say when it come to the toast, but he said, 'I know what to say. I've made speeches.'

He has. He done the vote of thanks one year at the South-West Midlands Motor Traders Association Annual Dinner, and he was in the toilet all afternoon with his nerves.

Anyway, he got to his feet, and he didn't fiddle with the tablecloth or read from anything. He just made a lovely little speech about being a dad, and how one minute you're pushing them in their pram and next thing you know you're walking them down the aisle of a church, and how glad he was Mel had inherited her mother's good taste in men. Of course, Scouser had to chime in then. He shouts, 'I don't know about that bit, Bradshaw,' and everybody laughed.

Andrew made a nice speech as well, but then he's used to it, standing up in court and everything. And Tim, his best man. Another lawyer. He's a toffee-nosed little runt. I seen him looking at Bobs' streaks. I seen him watching to see if he knew what knife and fork to use. I hope Mel never wants a divorce because there'd be nothing left but a little pile of bones by the time that lot had finished with her.

Audrey said to me, 'It'll do them both good to get away and relax. Get some good Scottish air. After all the fuss.' I think she might have been taking a pop at our wedding arrangements, only she always puts a little smile on when she talks to you so you can never be sure how to take her.

I must admit, I have seen brides look happier, but it's just Mel's way. You don't very often catch Melody with a smile on her face. She's always been the same. Even the day she learned to ride her bike and Bobs told her the flags'd be out in town, and they were because it was St George's Day, she had a face like thunder. Not like Roxy. Always chuckling.

I had a dance with John Godbold, and one with Mr Liquorish. I don't know where Mr Ives got to. I think he might be dead. And I seen Scouser trying to jive with Audrey. He mouthed to me, 'You're next.' That's what he thought. Once I've danced my obligations, I dance with my husband, and well he knows it. Mary's not much of a dancer. She was hanging round the gift display, trying to see who'd spent what.

Bobs said, 'You've done a brilliant job on this, Ba. You've done us all proud. Showed them Godbolds the Bradshaws know how to put on a spread. Showed them Andrew's made a good match.'

I said, 'How did you get on down your end, with Audrey and Hooray Henry?'

He said, 'Great. We got on great. He talks like a bit of a dipstick, but he can't help that. His dad's a judge. I told him I hoped he'd put a word in for me when my case comes up. He said he was sure I could afford a good brief. He's all right.'

Bobs always thinks the best of people. Heart as big as a house. That's his trouble half the time. He don't see things.

He said, 'Course, I upset Mel. On the way out to the car, coming to the church. I told her to leave her key on the hall table on the way out.'

I said, 'She was nervous. You can't expect people to see jokes when they're nervous.'

He said, 'Who said anything about jokes. She's a married woman now. She don't need to come barging in our place without an invitation.'

I never thought I'd hear such a thing from him. He might have done it to Jason, but not Melody.

He said, 'Time to move on, Ba. We've done our job. You wouldn't expect to have a key to their place, so why should they have a key to ours. We want the place to ourselves.'

I said, 'We've got a key to Jason and Diane's.'

He said, 'That's for watering plants. Don't split hairs with me, woman. I should have thought you'd like the idea of having your home back to yourself.'

And it's funny, because I'd have thought so, too. Only it just felt flat. I'm all right, though. I'm fine. I might offer to help out at the yard a bit more now

I haven't got weddings to worry about. And there's the grandchildren.

Then Jennifer Godbold was beckoning us from the edge of the dance floor. She said, 'I think Roxy might have cut herself and I can't find her mummy anywhere. I think she's changing the baby.'

She was sitting at the table, cuddling the bridal bunny Andrew had given her. She looked like she could do with an early night. She said, 'Look, Grandad, pink spit.' And she dribbled pink froth onto her serviette.

Bobs said, 'Has she had red pop? She must have been drinking red pop.'

But we hadn't had red pop. I said, 'Open your mouth wide, Roxanne, so Nana Ba can have a good look inside.' And there it was. Blood from her gums. Top, bottom, everywhere.

She said, 'I haven't had red pop. I've had lemonade, and a little taste of my daddy's champagne. I only had a little taste.'

Bobs said, 'There you are then. Champagne does funny things to people. Look at your Uncle Scouser. He's only had one glass and he's doing the Twist.'

She said, 'Yeah. I think it'll be all right, Grandad.'

I expect it will be all right.

He said, 'Now don't say anything. Just hear me out.'

This was what I was afraid of, once Melody was off the scene. I had a feeling he'd be bringing all that business up again.

He said, 'Let me just show you. Half an hour. There's nobody going to know, only you and me.'

I'm a broad-minded woman. Gays don't bother me. Mary thinks they should all have electric shocks, but they don't bother me. But I've never heard of anything like this. After thirty years of marriage.

I said, 'If you're turning into a woman, where does that leave me?'

He said, 'I'm *not* turning into a woman. I just want to put some of my gear on and sit with you for half an hour. I should be able to do that in my own home. I work hard enough.'

So that's what it's come down to. He's going to say

he can do as he pleases because he pays the bills. I'm not having that. Not now. He's always said, 'You do work, Ba. You look after all of us, and that's the most important job in the world.' I could get a job. I shall have to if he carries on like this.

He said, 'Just half an hour. That's all I'm asking. It's been hard for me, Ba, only doing it when I've had the place to myself. Specially lately. Sometimes you've just got to do things and hope they work out.'

I put the telly on, but I couldn't tell you what I watched. I could just hear him creaking about upstairs, putting tights on and ruining a good marriage. I've seen men like that on documentaries. Wearing sequins and too much Pan-stik. Singing 'Hey Big Spender' down in Soho, and telling blue jokes.

He said, 'I'm coming in. Are you ready?' but I never answered him, and I didn't look properly neither, not for quite a few minutes. I could see him out of the corner of my eye. I could see black and white. And then I turned my head a bit, and started with his feet. K shoes. Or Van-dam wide fitting. Black leather with a gilt and patent detail and a low heel. And then a black pleated skirt and a white blouse with a floppy bow at the neck. I've never seen anything so daft.

He said, 'Well? Not as bad as you thought, is it?'

He'd got lipstick on, and a bit of eye shadow, but nothing else. Pearl earrings.

I said, 'Where's the sequins?'

He said, 'I'm not a drag act, Ba. I'm not going to be doing the clubs.'

I said, 'So what's the point of it?'

He said, 'I just want to look nice. I don't want to be a laughing stock.'

I said, 'I should have thought if you were going to do it you'd have made a good job of it. I shouldn't have thought it'd be worth wrecking your marriage just to look like you work in Marshall and Snelgrove's cardigan department.'

And then he just sat there, watching the telly with his great big K shoes poking out in front of him, as if it was any normal night at home. So that's it. I'm phoning up and getting an appointment with that new lady doctor, because if he don't hurry up and get some tablets I'm going to need some.

The doctor was very nice. She don't look much older than our Melody, but she's done all her exams and she'd got her certificates up on her wall.

She said it's not all that unusual: married men dressing up. She said a lot of them do it in secret, and some of them get their wives to go along with it. Not round here, they don't.

She said there weren't really any tablets, not even for me. She said counselling would be the best thing. Everything's blummin' counselling these days. And she asked had I tried underwear. She said some men are happy if they can just wear some frillies under their trousers and nobody need be any the wiser. So that's how we left it. She was very nice. She said to feel I could go and talk to her about it any time. I mentioned Roxy as well, about her gums, and she said she ought to have a check-up, but I know Diane's doing that anyway. And she checked my blood pressure. Nothing wrong with me. I'm not the one that's got problems.

The way things worked out, Tiger Lil was having her first run for us at Brighton three days before Mary's birthday. So the plan was, the four of us pile down there, making out we were just having a day at the races, and then Mary gets the big surprise. I've never known Scouser keep a secret for so long. And then all the way down, Bobs was driving and they were in the back, she kept going on about what problems me and Bobs had had with Nice Little Runner, how she thought we'd have lost our taste for punishment, good money thrown after bad and all that, which was perfectly true, if I'm honest, but still I did feel sorry for Scouser, sitting on his big secret.

She was so busy prattling I thought she might not notice Bobs was pulling into the Owners and Trainers car park instead of Day Ticket Holders, but she did. She said, 'Is it running, then? I didn't know it was running. I thought you said it had got bad feet?'

Bobs said, 'No. It's one I'm thinking of buying. I've been down to see her working, and she's running today. I've took an option on her. See how she goes today. We're as good as decided though, aren't we, Ba?'

She said, 'And I thought you'd learned your lesson. You'll never be able to retire, you know? You'll be going out scrubbing floors, Barbara, if he keeps this up. Racehorses.'

First thing Scouser done when we'd parked was run to the lav. Bobs went and fetched the badges to get us in, and the race cards, and then we went up to the seafood bar and got crab salad and a bottle of Chardonnay. Course, Bobs weren't drinking, and I weren't really drinking in case he forgot he weren't drinking and I ended up having to drive, and Scouser said he'd have been happier with a Guinness, but we finished the bottle somehow.

Bobs said, 'Must be nearly your birthday, Mary. What's he got lined up for you this year?'

She said, 'Oh it's a big secret. He's taking me on a mystery trip, aren't you, Douglas?'

Scouser said, 'Oh look. There's that actor. Off *London's Burning*. Is it him? Don't everybody look round at the same time. Did I tell you I seen Dustin Hoffman this week? In Redditch. I'm sure it was him. If it weren't him it was his twin.'

Mary leaned over to me and whispered, 'He thinks I don't know, but I'm pretty sure he's taking me on the Eurostar.'

Tiger Lil was running in the 2.35. I did know that much. But I hadn't looked through the race card because I knew, if I did, she would, and I wanted Scouser to have his big moment. Then Bobs said, 'Are we bothering with the first race? I'd just as soon get a cup of tea and then go straight down to the parade ring for our race.'

But Mary said, 'Well, give me a minute to look at what's running. What's this one called that you might be buying? Lily the Pink? You want to buy a horse that's got a really good name. You want to get one called Streak of Lightning.'

So she found it on the card, but she didn't notice what she was supposed to notice, and then I looked. He was watching me, with a silly smile on his face, waiting for me to realize.

He said, 'Did you see who the owners are, Mary?' but she'd turned the page. She was looking to see if any greys were running in the big race. Mary always backs greys. He said, 'Have a look. I think it's somebody you'll be interested in.' Scouser had lost his tongue. Then she'd lost hers. She just kept reading it over and over.

She said, 'What does it mean, Douglas?'

He said, 'What does it say?'

It said it was owned by Mrs M. Vickery and Mrs B. Bradshaw. That's what it said.

Scouser said, 'Happy birthday, darling. You're a racehorse owner now. Well, half owner.'

She said, 'Half a racehorse. How much did it cost?'

I gave Bobs a bit of a cuddle. I said, 'It's not *my* birthday.'

He said, 'No, sweetheart. You're just my little investment opportunity. I always knew you'd have your uses some day, if I just hung on to you long enough.'

Mary said, 'Is it a grey?' which it wasn't, but she soon got over that, and then it was like somebody had knocked a hole in the blummin' Aswan dam. We couldn't get down to that parade ring fast enough. Never mind about the first race. We wanted to be down there, getting a look at her and behaving like proper owners.

She took my arm, and she said, 'I knew Douglas was up to something. I did have a suspicion.' But she never did.

The mist was clearing and the sun was breaking through. We went into the ring as soon as the runners in the first race had gone down to the start, and hung about, waiting for Mack. I said to Bobs, 'If I'd known I might be on the telly I wouldn't have worn this.'

He said, 'The telly people aren't here today. Anyway, if she wins, it'll be Mary in the spotlight. That's the deal. Next time she runs it'll be your turn. You're taking turns, and if we time it right it'll be your turn the day she wins the Oaks. Anyway, you look lovely. If I seen you on my telly I'd think, Who's that gorgeous woman? That mature but gorgeous creature. What wouldn't I give to have a woman like that in my bed? That's what I'd think.'

See? That's how he's always been. He's always said nice things. I couldn't have a better husband. If it weren't for this silly business.

I'm not convinced she's got the right name, Tiger Lil. She's got a real dopey look about her. Looked like she could hardly be bothered walking round the parade. And the rest of them were all frisking and whinnying, first time out for some of them.

We'd got a little apprentice riding her, Des Fogarty, and he was wearing Bradshaw colours, royal and yellow diabolo with emerald and yellow diabolo sleeves and quartered cap, because the Vickerys haven't got their own racing colours. Mary said something to him about the weather, but I don't think he could understand her cut-glass Brummy. Then she says to Scouser, loud enough for everybody to hear, 'He's not very big, is he? Couldn't you get a bigger one?'

Mack said he'd have liked a bit of rain overnight

for her. He said she liked a bit of cut in the ground. Mary says to me, 'It's very complicated, isn't it? We shall have to gen up on it. You'll have to show me how to put a bet on. You'll have to tell me what to say to the tic-tac man.' Bobs done a sign to me, on the quiet. I said, 'What's that? Nine to Four?' He says, 'No. Thick as brick.'

Him and Scouser ran across to the betting ring and put their money on with Ted Salmon, but I took Mary to the Tote and she splashed out four pounds to win, and I done a dual forecast with Big Noise From Winnetka.

I don't know about anybody else, but my guts were churning. It might have been the crab, but I think it were seeing Des Fogarty up there on the monitor in my Bobs' colours. Anyway, she went into that starting gate like an angel and she come out of it like a piece of wet soap. She was all over the place, though. I didn't think the lad was going to have time to settle her, but once they were in the straight something seemed to click with her. She put her head down and King's Ransom and Noches Estrelladas were out the back door. I thought Bobs and Scouser were going to fall out of the stand. And Mary was shouting, 'Which one's ours? Which one's ours?' She was second, by a neck, to Big Noise, so the Ted Salmon Bookies Benevolent Fund got a nice cash injection, and the Tote owed me sixty-four pounds twenty thank you very much.

Bobs said, 'I don't know what your plans are, Vickery, but I'm going home with this one. She's got petrol money.' In fact, by the end of the afternoon I'd got more than petrol money. I had Canada Dry for a place in the 3.35 and she went off at 100/1, and then I took Mary down, before the 4.15, to show her how to have a proper bet, because she was feeling a bit flat about our girl getting pipped at the post. She had a little bet on Pinogrigio because it was a grey, and Gus Demmy was offering 12/1 on Aziza Aziza, so I thought I'd have some of that.

I said, 'Any news from your Fleur? Is she coming over?'

She said, 'Nothing definite. She's so busy. She's got a message service, of course, but we don't often get time for a chat. And they've bought a boat, did I tell you? So bang goes their weekends. We'll probably go there. I'll ring her tonight anyway. Tell her about the horse. I don't suppose Douglas has told her. It must be nice for you, having them nearby. Having them drop in. Seeing the kiddies.' Poor old Mary. I do feel sorry for her sometimes.

We stopped off at a place on the river near Oxford and had roast mallard and passion-fruit ice cream for afters. It was gone nine when we got back and the phone was ringing.

Diane said, 'Where've you been? I've been trying to get you since three.'

So I started telling her all about Mary's birthday surprise and everything.

But she said, 'I can't listen to you, Mum. Roxy's tests have come back and they think it's leukaemia. She's got to go in on Monday and have her marrow tested. They've told us they'll have to drill into her hip bone and Jason's gone all to pieces.'

I said I'd have Blair and Bobs said he'd look after Jason's office, but Diane said no need because Jason wouldn't be going with them. He's always been funny about hospitals. Even visiting for half an hour he comes over faint.

Bobs said, 'I'll make him come over faint. Not going to the hospital when your kiddie's got to have needles stuck in her. I've never heard anything like it. You've been too soft with him, Ba. Always were.'

I could see that coming a mile off. But I'm not taking the blame for a twenty-nine-year old. Diane's had him long enough now to have sorted him out. And she has, in many ways. He'll eat mushrooms now, and he never would for me. Anyway, it don't matter. Roxy's what matters. I said to him, 'It might be better if he's not there, if he's going to faint. She might be better off just having Diane with her.'

He said, 'Well he can go after they've finished with the needles. Be there when she wakes up. Take her a little dolly in or something. He's not sitting in that office all day pretending nothing's wrong.'

See, this is Bobs all over. Once he's decided something, everybody's expected to fall in behind him. And really *he'd* like to be at the hospital. Needles wouldn't bother him.

Diane dropped Blair off about half-past seven, because they'd got to be at the clinic before nine and there's always tailbacks down the Hagley Road. Roxy was in the back in a little red T-shirt.

Bobs said, 'And where do you think you're going, young lady?'

She said, 'I've got to have a little operation. I've got to go to sleep, and when I wake up it'll be all over. And I've got to have platelets, Grandad. You can't see them because they're very very tiny. Have you ever had platelets?'

He said, 'No. But I have heard they make you feel better. I have heard that girls who sit nice and still for the platelet doctor get to go for a drive to see their nana's new horse.'

Blair was grizzling for Diane, and I could see she wanted to be off. She said she'd phone us, once she knew a bit more. She said, 'Course, it might not be anything. She might just be a bit run-down.'

Bobs took Blair for a jog round the garden and got him laughing at the windmill while I done him some Ready Brek, and then we had a cup of tea.

He said, 'If today goes all right for Roxy, I might pop out for an hour tonight.'

I thought he meant pop round to the hospital.

I said, 'She'll be too tired for visitors, Bobs. They'll have her doped up.'

He said, 'No. I didn't mean that. There's a thing I thought I'd go to. A meeting.'

I said, 'Trade?' but I knew it weren't. There's no trade meetings in August.

He said, 'No, not trade. The other.'

The other.

I said, 'I don't believe I'm hearing this. Our Roxy's got leukaemia and all you can think about is dressing up in frocks.'

He said, 'It's not *all* I think about.'

I said, 'Five minutes ago you was playing peep-bo round the door with your little grandson.'

He said, 'That's got nothing to do with anything. What I do isn't going to make any difference to Roxy getting better. These are separate things, Ba. I can be a grandad and wear dresses. If you don't want me to go tonight, I won't go. But that's just tonight. Sooner or later I will go.'

I told him to go. I don't want him sitting here,

changing channels every blummin' minute, wishing he was there. And if he does it there perhaps he won't want to do it here. Get it out of his system. That's the way I've got to look at it.

I said, 'Please yourself. I've got more important things on my mind.'

He said, 'Oh well, I've only got two businesses to run and a granddaughter poorly in hospital, so I'll just be sitting on my arse all day reading *Vogue*.'

I hate it when he drives off in a paddy and we're not speaking.

Mary was a good pal. Phoned up to see if I wanted any shopping doing, save me struggling round Sainsbury's with a pushchair. Then Melody pitched up here on an early lunch. Says her marriage is over. Apparently Andrew sits reading files when he comes home instead of watching telly with her, and he says eggs shouldn't be kept in the fridge and she says they should.

I said, 'It'd be nice if you'd give a thought to somebody else for five minutes. She's having her bone marrow done today. A little dot like that having bits drilled out of her.'

She said, 'I'm not listening. I don't want to hear anything about insides.'

I said, 'Have you phoned your brother?'

I put Blair's changing mat on the work top next to the sink. She said, 'Ah, God, you're not going to

117

do that in the kitchen, are you?' I should have made her do it. I said, 'You ought to be doing this. Have a little practice. You'll be doing this one fine day. He's lying here good as gold.'

Blair don't know it, but I think he saved the day. If she hadn't seen me changing his nappy and the kitchen all cluttered up with his stuff I think she'd have been talking about moving back in. She cleared off back to the boutique, anyway. It's like I told her. You've got to work at marriage. You don't throw it all away over where you should keep eggs.

I said, 'Phone your brother. Tonight.'

There was no word from Diane, but I left here about half-past twelve so I could cover the phones while people were on their lunch hours and Bobs could get over to Rowley and take over from Jason. He never said much. Not in front of staff. Things were pretty quiet and Blair nodded off, so I had a little look round, see if I could find out what this meeting was he was so keen on going to. There was nothing in his desk diary, though. Just a suit-carrier in the back of a cupboard with a camel scoop-neck top and skirt and two pairs of nubuck sling-backs, one taupe, one ivory, still in their boxes, mail order from somewhere called Cross Purposes, never been worn.

There was nothing for me to do. I could have stopped home, but I wouldn't have settled to anything there neither. He'd said PDJ might phone about their fleet contract, and he'd left a Dulux chart so I could pick a new colour for his walls. Mick was out, bringing in a Lancia that was upside down in a ditch, and the paint-sprayers were busy. I tidied his plants up a bit and then sat with my magazine. There was one of them quizzes. Are you a Thinker, a Feeler or a Doer? I only went in his desk to find a pen because my bag was next to the pushchair and I didn't want to wake the bab.

There was lipsticks and all sorts in there. Mascara. Rings and necklaces, and little chiffon scarves. And addresses. Some place in London. Eversholt Street. And somewhere in Handsworth. Transformation, that's all it said, and then a little map, somewhere near the West Brom ground and this address. I jotted it down. Just in case. Because you never know. Like they say on *Crimewatch*, it's the details that can make the difference.

It was that stifling in there, even with the fan on. We needed a thunderstorm really. Anyway, about four, I was just thinking of taking Blair out and getting him an ice cream when he rang. He said, 'It's not good news, but it's not the worst. She's got something called ALL and one of the Ls stands for leukaemia. But they've told Diane she's got a very good chance. They've got this treatment and it usually knocks it on the head.'

I said, 'Where's Jason?'

He said, 'He's gone. I told him to get straight down there and never mind about anything else. Are you all right?'

I said, 'I feel blummin' useless.'

He said, 'I know. I asked Diane about us getting her in somewhere private. I said we'd bung. But she said private wouldn't gain her anything. They're starting her treatment tomorrow, and Di says they really know what they're doing. So I suppose we just hang on to the tiddler, keep him with us tonight, and wait till we can go and visit. Get Mick or Kevin to switch the phones over and close up and I'll see you at home.'

I said, 'I thought you were going out?'

He said, 'No. Don't seem right. Not tonight. I'll maybe go next week.'

I said, 'Go if you want to. You might not be able to next week. Things might be worse next week.'

I could tell he was weighing it up and I couldn't be bothered arguing any more. There's obviously been more going on than I know about, and if he wants to go off having secret meetings when our Roxy's at death's door he's the one's got to live with his conscience. We can manage without him. Me and Diane'll get her through it. And Jason.

I hadn't been in many minutes. I was just doing Blair a boiled egg and bread-and-butter soldiers and Scouser turned up with two big packs of disposables. I'd told Mary there was no hurry.

He said, 'Guess who I've just seen?'

Scouser's always seen somebody. He likes you to try and guess, and then it's always somebody that's not been on the telly for years and you'd never guess if you stood there all night.

I said, 'Not today, Scouser. I'm not in the mood.'

He said, 'Ray Reardon. Snooker? You remember? He was in Superdrug buying fly spray.'

Scouser seen Shirley Bassey once, coming out of that butcher's at the Holly Bush.

He said, 'Any news from the hospital?' and I don't know what come over me. I'd been all right till then, but once I'd started I couldn't stop. I told him there was tissues, but he fetched me a mile of toilet roll and gave me one of his big bear-hugs. There weren't any call for that, but Scouser never needed much encouragement. Still, I was glad to have him there.

He said, 'Where's Bradshaw?' and I said, 'On his way home,' just so he didn't get any big ideas.

He said, 'Well, you put the kettle on and I'll have a go at this,' and he got Blair's bib on and a spoon or two of egg into his mouth before Blair started wondering who he was and holding his arms out for me. Credit where it's due, though, he got most of it into him, and when Blair seen him scoffing his soldiers he decided he wanted them as well. Then they had a Mr Men yoghurt, and that's more than I've ever seen Blair eat.

He said, 'You've got to think positive, Ba. They can do wonders these days. Remember that little lad they had the collection for at the John Barleycorn? Remember they had that big jar of coins on the bar? He had leukaemia.'

I do remember it. That jar got took when they was burgled.

He said, 'He's as right as rain now. Must be ten or eleven. Great strapping lad. You'd never think.'

I said, 'But there's different kinds of leukaemia. I don't even know what she's got yet. I don't know anything. I wish Diane'd ring.'

And she did. I'd no sooner said it and there she was.

She said, 'Are you coming in to see her tonight? She keeps asking.'

I said, 'I didn't think we'd be allowed. I thought we'd have to leave it till tomorrow.'

She said, 'They'll be starting her treatment tomorrow. Tonight would be better. I'll get Jason to fetch Blair. Is he all right?'

I said, 'Yes. His Uncle Scouser just gave him his tea and I don't know who's got more yoghurt down their chin.' I didn't know what to say about Bobs.

I said, 'Dad's not back yet. I think he's got a meeting. But if Jason fetches the bab, I'll come and see her.'

Then I'd got Scouser talking in one ear and Diane in the other. He said, 'I'll babysit. Save Jason any bother. Tell her I'll sit with him till you get back.' And Diane said, 'I'll see if I can catch Dad at the office. She keeps asking when her grandad's coming in.' I just hoped he weren't already on his way to Handsworth, dressed like Princess Anne.

She didn't look too bad, considering. She was on a drip with the curtains closed round her, but she were as bright as a button. Bobs turned up with a parcel for her, of course. He'd got her a pair of Forever Friends pyjamas.

He said, 'Now I don't want you wearing these out. Shuffling round in that bed wearing a hole in the bum. I want you up and out of that bed, quick sticks.'

She said, 'Grandad! I've got to have injections. It's called Christine and it might make my legs wonky for a bit.'

It's called vincristine. She's got to have an injection once a week and tablets every day, but she'll be off the drip by Wednesday.

Me and Diane went for a little walk while Bobs were larking around with Roxy.

She said, 'She's in for a rough passage, Mum. She's

got to have injections in her spine and all sorts. You should see some of the kiddies in here. There's a little boy in a side room, no hair and white as a sheet. I was talking to his Gran, and she said you only get one bite of the cherry. She said if it comes back it's always worse, and it's their third time.'

I said, 'Well, we'll look after Blair, so don't worry about him. You just concentrate on getting Roxy through this. How's Jason feel about it?'

She said, 'He's bloody useless, that son of yours.'

I've never heard Diane use language like that before.

Roxy didn't want us to leave. She was hanging round my neck saying, 'I want to come home with you.' In the end I said to Bobs, 'One at a time, being as we're in separate cars.' So he went first, waving and doing silly walks, but I could see he was choked up, and then I gave it another five minutes.

When I got home, him and Scouser were having a beer. The tea things were still in the kitchen, egg yolk set hard, and all Blair's teddies and the bits out of his Bizzy Bee play box were strewn across the lounge.

Scouser said, 'He's a little tyke, isn't he?'

Later on, after he'd gone, Bobs said, 'He was out like a light when I got back. Flat on his back on the settee, with Blair asleep on top of him.'

I said, 'You decided not to go out, then?'

He said, 'Next time. It's once a fortnight. I might just dress a little bit at night when I come home. I'll stay upstairs so you don't see, if you like. I'm not forcing you to see it.'

I said, 'I'm not interested. I'm only interested in our Roxy getting better.'

He said, 'Course. And I've made a decision. I'm going to start saying a little prayer. Last thing at night. Any time really. Can't do no harm.'

We didn't get to bed till nearly midnight. I'd forgotten what time you have to get up when there's a baby in the house.

Audrey Godbold wrote to say how sorry they were to hear, and was there anything they could do to help. I did think Melody and Andrew might offer a bit of baby-sitting. We're getting too old for babies all day long, and Diane's mum's in New Zealand and she's never offered to fly over. Scouser and Mary have sat with him a few times. Like Mary says, she might as well get in training, in case their Fleur gets broody. Bobs reckons it's neck and neck between Fleur and that blummin' panda at London zoo.

Anyway, on the Monday I'd got the gas people putting the new boiler in, so one of Di and Jason's neighbours had Blair for the day. Roxy was having her second injection as well. We got a shock when we seen her. Diane had told us her hair was starting to go, but it weren't just that. She just sat there, hardly said a word, and her face looked all podgy and her little legs are getting like matchsticks. Diane looks all in. The family she'd got friendly with, that had the boy who was so poorly, they've gone. They've let him go home. And it's a little Paki girl in the next room so, of course, her Mum don't speak the lingo. Jason has been going in a bit more, though.

He said, 'You know what I'm like with hospitals, Mum.'

Diane's roots need doing. I told her to make an appointment and I'd sit with Roxy. Audrey Godbold wouldn't mind baby-sitting. She keeps offering. I think she's hoping for grandchildren. I think she's starting to realize she could have a long wait till Melody comes up trumps. Or Scouser'd do it. He's been grand. Mary don't mind. She won't do nappies or anything, but she don't mind tagging along.

Two more injections and then they have another look at her bone marrow. And that's not the end of it. There's weeks of treatments. Months. I don't think we shall know if she's in the clear this side of Christmas.

Bobs come in at teatime and brought her a Spirograph, but she's not well. She hardly wants to be bothered with anything. She was lying there watching *Blue Peter*. They've got this appeal going. Hearing Friends. Dogs for deaf people. Anyway, he got it out the box and started playing with it. He kept saying, 'This Spirograph's brilliant. I think I might take it home and keep it.'

She said 'Grandad! I will play with it. I'm just keeping my eye on the Totalizer at the moment.'

He said, 'I'll be out tonight, Ba. You know? Shouldn't be late back though.'

I said, 'Be as late as you like. And don't talk about that business in here.'

We kept our voices right down and there was a brass band playing on *Blue Peter*, but after he'd gone Roxy said to me, 'Nana, why are you cross with Grandad?'

I wished then I hadn't said anything. She might be poorly, but her ears never stop flapping.

Anyway, I dropped round Mel and Andrew's on the way back. We had a bit of quiche and salad and then Andrew had got papers to work on for the morning, so me and Mel watched *Steel Magnolias* and had a good cry.

I said, 'Roxy liked the card you sent her. You should see all the cards she's had sent.'

Mel said, 'We will go and see her. Once she's home.'

But I said, 'That won't be for a while. She's got injections to have still, and then she'll have a tube. You won't like that. Going under her skin and into her chest. You ought to go and see her now and not be such a big baby.'

They've got their place quite nice now. Old-fashioned, but I suppose it's good quality. Little tables.
Things from his side. All right, if you like that kind
of thing. You'd think they'd like something a bit more
with it, just starting out. Something a bit smarter.
Not old granny stuff like that.

I seen his tail lights as I turned in the drive. He was sitting writing a note. First thing I thought was, Roxy.

I said, 'What's happened? What's happened? She was all right when I left.'

He said, 'Nothing's happened. I've just brought Blair's babywalker round. I did say I'd bring it.'

He did. I'd clean forgot.

He was just getting it out of the boot when Bobs pulled in. Angora wrap-over jumper and double-drop pearl earclips. I remember thinking he actually looked quite nice. I suppose it's never such a shock as the first time. But then he seen Jason, and Jason looked at him, and I thought my poor old heart was going to jump out of my chest. If he'd only thought when he seen Jason's car, he could have backed out. Gone for a drive round for half an hour. If I'd only thought, I could have made something up, about Bobs doing it for a dare or something. But there weren't any time.

Bobs' window come down and he started asking about Roxy, same as I did. But Jason was just looking and looking, and fumbling, trying to get back in his car without taking his eyes off his dad. All he said was, 'You sick bastard.' And he drove off. His boot lid was still up and he went that fast you could see his tyre marks the next morning.

Bobs got out. Flared skirt. Ivory with flowers on it, and bronzy-coloured sandals, like plaited leather. He said, 'Oh well,' and then he carried the baby-walker in the house, but only the frame and the base. Jason had drove off with the little seat still in the boot.

I wanted to phone him, but Bobs said, 'Leave it. Let him go home and think about it before you start bending his ear.'

I didn't want him *thinking* about it. But it was late. And I didn't really know what I was going to say to him, so I decided I'd leave it till the morning, and just hope he hadn't gone bothering Diane with it. There's no sense in making complications. Getting everybody talking about it, stirring up trouble, and then Bobs might have got it out of his system and nobody need have knowed. I think that's the best way. Let him get it out of his system and then get back to normal. Have a little holiday and put it all behind us, once Roxy's on the mend. It's just a pity him and Jason had to bump into one another like that. Another five minutes and Jason would have been gone. Anyway, he wouldn't tell Diane. He keeps things close to his chest. Jason's not one for making a fuss.

Some day we'll look back on all this and laugh.

It got to nearly eight o'clock. I must have wiped that kitchen over twenty times, all the worktops, draining board, cupboard fronts. He was sat there, still in his robe, like he didn't have a job to go to, and I didn't want to say anything. Didn't want to start anything. I wanted him dressed and out before Jason brought Blair. I didn't want a shouting match, upsetting the nipper. And I thought if I could have five minutes with Jason, try and explain things to him, I could maybe smooth it over before he said anything to Diane or Melody.

I was just cleaning the crumb tray off the toaster when I heard his car. He come in, no Blair, and he walked across to Bobs and thumped him. Never said a word, never looked at me. Just walked across to his dad, smacked him on the nose, and walked out again. Bobs got up, pushed his chair back and started to go after him, and by the time he got round the table his nose was bleeding and Jason had turned round and come back for him.

He said, 'You effing, effing pervert,' and then he punched him hard in the privates. Bobs were doubled up, nose dripping blood, and then Jason started shouting, jabbing at his dad with his finger. He said, 'You stay away from my family, you effing bastard. We don't want nothing more to do with you. And don't go near that effing hospital else I'll break your effing legs.'

I said, 'Jason, if you'll just listen to me for a minute,' but he said, 'And you're as bad as he is, putting up with it. He wants chucking out. He wants locking up.' Then he said a terrible thing. He said, 'I'm warning you. I'm taking Blair to the doctor's this afternoon, and if there's any sign he's been interfered with there won't be any messing about with effing social workers. I shall just be straight round here with a sharp knife.'

There was no talking to him. I mean, even I know they don't interfere with kiddies, but he wouldn't listen to anything. He just effed a bit more and went.

I fetched a bag of frozen peas for Bobs' nose. He'd got his head in his hands.

He said, 'He's not going to stop me seeing them kiddies. He's not going to stop you neither.'

I said, 'I wouldn't be too sure about that.' I hate

to see a man cry, but to tell the truth I could have strangled him, and I've been feeling like that ever since he started all this business. He's spoiled every-thing.

I said, 'Well, I'm going up that hospital today. See Diane. And I don't want you turning up, wrecking everything. You've just got to leave it to me now, Bobs, and hope I can talk Jason round. And you've got to give him time.'

He said, 'I know that. And I know'd it'd come to this. Had to. It's just Roxy. I don't want Jason telling her he's banned me. I don't want her fretting. If Diane lets you see her you can make out I've had to go away for a bit. Tell her Grandad's had to go away on busi-ness. Give it a few days and then he might see reason.'

A few days! See, he still don't get it. He's twisted it round in his own mind that this dressing business is all right, and he don't have an inkling what it feels like when you find out. It's like he's in a dream. Thinking Jason's going to be all right in a few days. Thinking everything can just carry on like before. And the damage is done now. Don't matter if he chucks every blummin' blouse and skirt on a bonfire today. It's too late. That's what I keep thinking, over and over. It's too late. He's dreaming he can make it all right, and he can't. He's in a dream and I'm in a flipping nightmare. And there won't be any end to it. It'll keep leaking out. Melody'll find out. And Mary. It'll be all round the golf club. All round the Rotary. I can't see any way out of it ever. And if it weren't for our Roxy I'd have closed my eyes, God forgive me, and drove into the back of that petrol tanker this morning.

The ward sister come darting out of her office. She said, 'Mrs Bradshaw? Could I have a word?' So she knows.

She said, 'Your daughter-in-law would like a moment with you. Why don't you sit in here and I'll tell her you've arrived?'

She knows, so it'll be all over the hospital and everybody that works there'll go home and tell somebody else. It'll be in the blummin' *Mail* by tomorrow.

Diane come along without the sister. She said, 'You've had a wasted journey. She's fast asleep.' She wouldn't even look me in the eye.

I said, 'Well if she's asleep I'll sit with her. Give you a break.'

She said, 'Jason don't want you to,' ever so quiet, then she said, 'Look, Mum, I'm caught in the middle here and I don't even really know what's going on.

Jason says he don't want you and Bobs visiting any more and he's talking about police and all sorts, and I can't even make out what you've done.'

I said, 'Has he said anything to Roxy?'

She didn't answer me for a minute. Then she said, 'I've got to tell her you've gone on holiday.'

I said, 'Who's got Blair?'

She said, 'Neighbour. Don't make it harder for me, Mum. Jason wouldn't do something like this without good reason. You'll have to talk to him.'

She was near to tears. I was near to tears. We've always got on, me and Diane. She's been like a daughter to me. Specially with her Mum being overseas. And she don't fly off the handle like Jason.

I said, 'Look, it's something and nothing. You know what Bobs is like, always fooling around. And sometimes he dresses up. It's for a lark more than anything. Like fancy dress. But Jason's got the idea there's something bad going on. He got the wrong impression, and if he'd calm down long enough for me to talk to him I could sort it out. We've got to sort it out, Di. You can't keep us away from the kiddies.'

She said, 'What do you mean, dresses up?' So I told her.

I said, 'See? It's just a stupid thing he does sometimes. But it don't make him a bad grandad. He's not evil, Di. You know that.'

Then she got up. She said, 'You're as bad as he is. I've never heard anything like it. Jason's right. I don't want you round my kids. What am I supposed to tell Roxy? Your grandad's not your grandad any more, he's your grandma? You're as bad as he is. Jason was right.'

I was still blarting when the sister come back. She said, 'I'll fetch us both a coffee and we can go and have a chat somewhere a bit quieter. I'll just tell my staff nurse where I'll be.'

I told her everything. I was past caring.

She said, 'Your son's probably worried he's going to go the same way.'

I said, 'Don't say that. Does it run in families?'

She laughed. She said, 'No it doesn't. But that's what people think when they first find out. You're not the first family this has happened to, you know?'

Well, obviously, I knew that. I do know a little bit about life.

She said, 'There's a lot of it goes on. We used to see a lot of it on Casualty. Men in suits wearing ladies knickers underneath. We had an MP brought in once, when I was at St Thomas's, stockings, red and black undies and everything under his suit.'

I said, 'My husband only wears nice things. He'd never wear anything like that.'

She said, 'Your son and his wife, they're under a

big strain. They're worried out of their minds about Roxanne, and now this has blown up. You might have to let them concentrate on Roxanne just for now, and give them time.'

I said, 'But that's the thing. We were doing our bit, visiting Roxy, helping out with the bab, and now Jason won't even let me do that.'

She said, 'People get a lot of funny ideas about cross-dressers. They get them mixed up with gays and paedophiles. They just lump them all together. Either that or they think they're all having sex changes on the NHS.'

Sex change? I hadn't even thought of that. I suppose she thought she was being helpful. I mean, it was nice to be able to talk to somebody. But *sex change*. I could have done without that to worry about.

She said, 'You should talk to someone. Another wife. Someone who's been through it.'

I said, 'Who?'

She said, 'No, I don't actually know anybody, but I could find out. I bet there's a help line.'

She's probably right. There's help lines for everything these days.

She said, 'Would you like me to find out?'

I said, 'If it's no trouble.' I'm not phoning no help line. Telling my business to strangers.

She said, 'And you can always phone, to ask about

Roxanne. Just phone the ward and we'll tell you how she's doing. Until you've patched things up with your son.'

I said, 'He couldn't get a sex change without asking me, could he?'

She said, 'Does he want one? He probably doesn't even want one.'

I don't know though, do I? I don't know anything any more.

He never come home last night. The phone were alive, only I just left the machine on and listened in. I was hoping Jason might call me, or Diane, but first it was Mack wanting to talk about running Tiger Lil next month, then it was Mary to say she'd just been chatting to *her* trainer, then Audrey Godbold wondering what the news was on Roxy. Wondering what the news was on her son's father-in-law wearing frocks, more like. I know there's a whole crowd of them do League of Friends at the hospitals, taking the library trolley round and selling cups of tea. She'll have heard. A story like that, they'll soon have had the tom-toms out.

It was nine o'clock before I heard from him. He said, 'Are you all right?'

I said, 'I've felt better.'

He said, 'Yeah, but are you all right?'

I said, 'Where are you?'

He said, 'I shan't be home. I thought it'd be best. Just for a night or two. Call me on the mobile if you need me.' And that was it. He rung off.

We haven't had many nights apart in thirty years. When I was in the nursing home having Jason and Mel he was like a little orphan. Couldn't get us home fast enough. And whenever he's been away on business he's always said he couldn't sleep. But everything's changed now. It's a good job you don't know when these things are on the way. We were happy as Larry until I found that frock.

I was sitting there, in the dark, wondering what to do about Scouser and Mary and our Melody, when it rung again and made me jump out of my skin. I was hoping it was him. Well, I was and I wasn't. I didn't really want to see him, and I didn't want to talk about it any more because we're never going to agree about it, not if we talk till Scouser's hair grows back. But I didn't like him not being there. I'd have liked to be able to hear him moving about.

Anyway, I answered.

She said, 'It's Chris Galloway. I've got you a phone number.'

I just couldn't think.

Then she said, 'It's Sister Galloway, from the Children's Hospital. I talked to my friend and she gave me a phone number for you. It's a kind of advice line.'

That was nice of her. She didn't have to do that.

I scribbled it down on the back of my magazine, just to be polite really. I'm not phoning no advice line.

I kept waking on and off all night, thinking he might have come home, and then this morning I thought, 'I've had enough of this. Jumping every time the phone rings. Frightened to nip out for a carton of milk.' I moved all my stuff down to Melody's old room, had a nice hot shower and a slice of melon, and then I phoned Mary. I said, 'I know it's your day for golf, but I need you.'

She said she'd see me in Café Dino at eleven, so that gave me just an hour.

I didn't bother calling to see if he'd be busy. I just drove down there, parked in a reserved space and went straight in. That little girl he's got in reception sat with her mouth open and nothing coming out. I said, 'You needn't bother buzzing him. He's always got time to see his mother.'

There he was, reading the back page of the *Express* and picking his nose. His mouth dropped open as well. That was two goldfish impressions already and the day was still young.

I said, 'Don't start. You can just keep quiet and

listen to me for a change.' Then he got that mardy look he used to give me when he was about three.

I said, 'You're not going to make my life a misery, Jason. If you've got a problem with your dad, sort it out with him, but I'm not having you blaming me, keeping me from seeing my grandkiddies. I'm not having it. And if you want a big scene down at that hospital, you can have one.'

He said, 'Have you chucked him out then?'

I said, 'That's my business. If you need to know something, I'll tell you. And don't be so nasty. After everything your dad's done for you.'

He said, 'How do you mean, *a big scene*?'

I said, 'If I get down that hospital and they tell me I'm still barred, I shall give them a day to remember. If I get treated like a blummin' criminal I shall behave like one. And if you're embarrassed about your dad, just try crossing me. I'll embarrass you.'

He said, 'It's up to Diane.'

I said, 'Three o'clock, Jason. I shall be there at three o'clock.'

Mary was waiting for me with two cappuccinos. She said, 'What's up? Is it Roxy?'

I said, 'No. She's doing as well as can be expected. It's Bobs. I'm divorcing him.'

I thought she was going to have a seizure. 'Oh, Ba,' she said. 'What a shock.'

That's all she kept saying. 'What a shock. What a shock.' Then it turned out it weren't such a shock after all. She was eating the top off her cappuccino with a spoon and she says, 'I mean Douglas has mentioned a few things. Just recently. He did say you didn't seem very happy. He did say he didn't think Bobs was pulling his weight, you know, with you having the baby to look after and everything?'

I said, 'Bobs has always pulled his weight.'

'Oh!' she says. 'Oh!'

I could see her trying to work that one out. As

soon as you mention divorce all they want to hear is dirt.

She said, 'Is it another woman?'

I said, 'Not exactly. Do you know what a transvestite is?' It was the first time I'd actually said the word. Funny how your voice suddenly seems really loud if you say a word like that in Café Dino.

She said, 'What? Men who have an operation?'

I said, 'No. Men who wear frocks. Bobs is a transvestite. So I'm divorcing him.'

She started laughing. She said, 'You're having me on. Was this Douglas's idea?'

I told her everything that had happened, but I could see she still weren't sure. She said, 'But he's such a big man. Where can he get high heels to fit a man his size?' I said, 'They have special shops. They're all over the place. Birmingham. Bristol. They've even got them in Newcastle. I was talking to somebody in the medical profession, and she said there's thousands of them. And a lot of them keep it a secret all their lives.' I said, 'It could just as easy be Scouser as Bobs.'

She said, 'Well I don't think so, Barbara. Not my Douglas.'

I hate it when she calls me Barbara. I said, 'Anyway, he's dead set on it, and they tell me it's one of them things that never goes away, so I'm getting a divorce.'

She said, 'What a shock. What does your Melody think about it?' I hadn't particularly thought about Melody, not with Jason playing such hell. One scrap at a time, that was the way I was working.

I said, 'Will you tell Scouser or will I?'

She said, 'Oh, I will. I'll tell him tonight. What a shock, though. He'll be ever so upset. All those years they've been friends. Bobs was his best friend.'

I said, 'Well, perhaps he still will be. Just because I'm divorcing him don't mean you can't still be friends with him.'

'Oh, no,' she said, 'I don't think so. Not if he's going to carry on like that. I mean, if I ever saw him, you know, like that, I'd just burst out laughing.'

I don't think she would, though.

She said, 'How will you manage?' She meant money, I suppose. I don't know. I'll work. I've never been afraid of work.

She said, 'I was wondering, about the horse?'

I said, 'Yes. Mack says he wants to give her another race.'

She said, 'Do you think you'll want to sell your half?'

You know them big ugly birds you see on the nature programmes, circling in the sky round some poor old zebra that's on his last legs? They're distant relations of Mary. Not all that distant neither.

I said, 'I haven't got any plans to. I wouldn't mind another day at the races.'

'Hm,' she said. 'You don't think Bobs would, you know, turn up, or anything?'

Roxy said, 'Where's my grandad?'

Diane was fidgeting about behind me. She never left me alone with her for a second. Jason's instructions, I suppose.

I said, 'He's had to go to London. He'll be back.'

She's got this Hickman line in her chest, now, to get the drugs into her. I think this might be the roughest stretch so far. Then, in September, there'll be something else, injections or X-rays, in case it's spread to her brain.

Sister Galloway warned me about that.

I read her a story from her *Naughty Little Sister* book, and then she played with my bracelets. I asked Diane who'd got Blair. She said, 'He's in the crèche. It's easier than all that to-ing and fro-ing to your place,' and she gave me a long hard look.

Roxy dozed off after a bit. That happens a lot since

she started this treatment. Diane motioned to me to go outside with her.

She said, 'It was Jason's doing. I'd still have let you come.'

I said, 'He had no business hitting his dad.'

She said, 'Well, he was upset. It's a bloody mess, Mum. She keeps asking for her grandad and I don't know what to tell her.' I got the feeling, while she was talking, that I'm getting the blame for everything. Bobs, and Jason, and Blair having to go to that crèche. It's probably my fault Labour got in.

I told her about the divorce and she gave me a little hug. She said, 'I can't understand why he's being so selfish. Of all the times to cause trouble. I'd have expected better of him. He could have waited till Roxy was better.'

I said, 'I don't know that he could have waited. I don't think it works like that. And I don't think he sees it as selfish. I think, to his way of looking at it, he's spent fifty years *not* being selfish and he's come to the end of his rope.'

She said, 'You seem to know a lot about it. You make it sound like he's entitled. So how come you're chucking him out?'

Good question.

I went down to have a look at Blair. He was grizzling. He's always grizzling. It's an awful thing to say, but I'm not sorry they've made other arrangements for him, because he can be a little misery. Melody was like that. You couldn't put her down for two minutes without her starting up. And struggling with that blummin' pushchair in and out of the car. I'm too old for it. I used to love having Roxy, but, of course, I was younger then, and they were happier days.

She was awake when I got back up to the ward.

She said, 'Nana? What's a pervert?'

I said, 'Oh, just somebody who acts silly. Only it's not a nice word. How are you getting on with your Spirograph?'

So she showed me some patterns she'd done and told me who all her cards were from. I don't like the colour of her. They reckon she's getting on great, but I don't know. When I told her I'd got to go she hung round my neck like a little limpet.

She said, 'You don't have to go, Nan, not if you haven't got to get Grandad's tea.'

I told her Tiger Lil might be running again. I said, 'Remember what Grandad said? About having all your injections like a good girl and getting better and coming to see her?'

She said, 'I *am* being a good girl.' Then she started crying. First time I've seen her cry since she's been in there.

She said, 'My hair's falling out, Nana.'

I said, 'But it's going to grow back. It's going to grow back lovely.'

She said, 'Does Grandad know my hair's falling out?'

I said, 'Course he does.'

She said, 'I can't come and see your horse with no hair. It might frighten her.'

I said, 'You don't want to worry about that. She's used to your Uncle Scouser and he's got a head like a ping-pong ball.'

I managed not to cry till I got outside. I sat in the car park for ten minutes and had a good blart. I had to do that before I could get myself together for the next job.

Then I drove round to Melody and Andrew's.

They'd got the Godbolds coming for dinner, I thought, That's nice. All that sweat and brass we put into the wedding and they've never asked us round. Not for a proper dinner. The table was all laid up, but there was no sign of Andrew.

Mel said, 'Did we know you were coming?' It smelled like lamb.

I said, 'I've got something to tell you.' I suppose it weren't very fair really, not when she'd got company arriving, but I'd just got to get it all over and done with.

She said, 'Is it about Roxy?'

I said, 'No, she's not doing too badly. Not that a visit from her Aunty Melody wouldn't help, mind you.' She was bashing up Cadbury's flakes to put on the top of a trifle. I said, 'It's about me and your dad. I'm divorcing him for unreasonable behaviour.'

I thought she was going to go for me with her rolling pin. She said, 'You can't do that to my dad. Where is he? I want to see him. *You're* the one that's unreasonable.'

I said, 'And I've got to tell you why, Mel. I can't just leave it at that.'

Course, then we had her old routine, shutting her eyes, shaking her head, shouting, 'I'm not listening! Where's my dad? I want to see my dad.' So I grabbed hold of her by the rolling pin and pushed her up against the fridge, with my face right up close to hers. That shut her up. I'm bigger than she is.

I said, 'Do you think I like this? After thirty years? Do you think I want all this at my time of life?'

She just kept shaking her head. Her eyes were full. I was probably hurting her arms.

I said, 'There are men who wear dresses. They're not poofters and they don't interfere with kiddies and they don't do nobody any harm, but when you find out you're married to one you want to crawl in a blummin' hole and die. And that's all there is to it, Mel. Your dad's started wearing dresses and I can't handle it no more.'

She started laughing. I know that does happen sometimes when you mean to be serious, but I weren't in no mood for it.

I said, 'You won't laugh when you see him. You

ask your brother. He's seen him in a jumper and skirt.'

That was when the Godbolds arrived.

I heard her start snivelling the minute she'd opened the door to them. 'It's all ruined. Everything's ruined.' And, of course, Audrey thought she meant the dinner. She said, 'Well, it smells lovely.' Then she seen me.

It had to come out. Maybe it weren't the right time. I don't know. I could have had them round to tea, I suppose. Told them over a few Fondant Fancies. As far as I can see, there isn't any way of people finding out that don't make you feel like something out of a freak show. He might not have wanted it this way. He might have wanted to tell people himself. But he dropped me in it. The minute Jason seen him he'd dropped me well and truly in it. So I told them. I stood there in our Mel's kitchen and just told them. They're churchgoers as well.

Audrey said, 'Didn't you used to know someone who was like that, John? Wasn't there a barrister?'

He said, 'Circuit judge. Way back. Retired now. Dead probably. Oh yes, it was common knowledge. Of course, there wasn't so much of it about in those days.'

Audrey said, 'There's more of everything these days. You poor dear. All this and the little one so poorly as well. My brother-in-law had a cousin, second cousin, who went that way, too. Years ago.'

John said, 'No, Audrey. He wanted a sex change. That's a different thing.'

I said, 'Completely different. Bobs don't want to go in for anything like that. It's just the frocks.'

That started Mel off again.

Audrey said, 'It may be a different thing, but I know it caused a lot of bad feeling. I know wills had to be rewritten.'

John said, 'Maybe we should go, dear? Leave Melody with her mother?'

She said, 'Yes, we'll go. We can get something on toast. You don't want to be bothered with us.'

Mel said, 'Yes, I do. I've made a trifle. She's just going, aren't you?'

I didn't want to stop anyway. Hanging round where I'm not wanted with Audrey Godbold calling me a poor thing. I'd still got things to do.

I phoned Mary and Scouser's when I got home. Mary answered. I said, 'Have you told him?'

She put her hand over the mouthpiece, but I could still hear every word she said. He said he didn't know what to say to me, and she said, 'Well, thank you very much, Douglas, for lumbering me with this one.' I hung up. I'd have thought better of Scouser, all the years we've been friends. No, I wouldn't. He always was a coward.

So that meant I'd lost my best friends, threatened

my son, and ruined my daughter's future, and it was still only half-past eight. I had a nice big cold glass of that Frascati wine and an oven-chip butty. Then I decided what I was going to do.

There was a letter from him next morning. Imagine that. I've known him forty-five years and he's never written me a letter in his life before. It said how much he loved me and he was sorry for all the trouble, and he'd like to come by on Saturday morning and try and work a few things out.

I thought, 'Nice one, Bobs. Come to your senses *now*, after I've told everybody I'm divorcing you and everything. You're going to make me look like a proper chump.' I mean, I'd like us to be back like the old times, but I don't see how we can. Anyway, I closed my eyes and had a long hard think about it while Courtney was doing my hair, and I come to the conclusion the only way round it was to move away. Sell up and go. Near enough so the kiddies can visit, but far enough for nobody to know about this silly business.

I drove straight home from the hairdresser's. I never go nowhere nor see no-one these days. I'm like one of them Caramel nuns.

Scouser phoned me just before teatime. He sounded like somebody had got his nuts in a bench vice. He said, 'You all right, Ba?'

I said, 'What do you think?'

He said, 'I never did think he was right for you. I always said you should have chose me.'

I said, 'Did you know?'

He said, 'No.'

He said it too fast. I said, 'You never had an inkling?'

He said, 'No. Not really.'

Not *really*. What kind of an answer is that? I should never have asked Scouser. He changes his story oftener than he changes his socks. He'd say anything.

I said, 'Well either you knew or you didn't.'

He said, 'No. We just larked around a couple of times. You know? Putting his Pat's stuff on and larking around. It was just a laugh, in the summer holidays. He done it for a dare really. You know what Pat used to be like. Threatening him if he ever went in her bedroom. It was only for a lark. Do you want me to come round? Mary's going to the pictures with some golfing pal.'

I said, 'How do you mean, come round?' and he laughed. I said, 'You're a gutless wonder, Vickery.' I hung up on him. He'll be round, though.

The evenings are the worst. We've always spent our evenings together. Bobs were never one for hanging around in boozers at night. We'd watch telly, and I might read a bit, true crime or UFOs or something like that, if he was on the treadmill or looking at his *Raceform Update*. But I can't read since he's been gone. I start thinking I can hear something moving about outside, and you don't want the windows all locked in this weather. I wish I had something to do. Audrey Godbold does tapestry.

I watched *Lucky Numbers*, *Brookside*, *Question of Sport*, and *Only Fools and Horses*. They were all repeats. I could put a brick through that screen when I think what the licence costs. I was mooching around, eating a bag of them little Milky Ways, and then I found a pile of old *Hello* mags under the telephone seat. Britt Ekland's downsizing her lifestyle, apparently, and Princess Caroline's been seen with Prince Ernst of Hanover.

I was just putting some towels in the washer when I heard his car. My blummin' heart was doing a tap dance. My own husband, and my heart was hammering away like that. He shouted, 'Ba, it's me,' and then he walked in. I screamed when I seen him, but not as loud as he screamed when he seen me.

He said, 'What's happened? What have you done?'

I said, 'Had my head shaved. What have you had done?'

He said, 'Oh my good God, Ba. Your lovely hair. Whatever for?'

I told him. I said, 'I'm keeping Roxy company till her hair grows back. So she won't be the only baldie in the family. She was crying about her hair. So I thought, "right".'

He said, 'You've seen her, then?'

He'd had Andrew round at the office to tell him

Melody was having a nervous breakdown.

He said, 'He tells me you're going after a divorce.'

I said, 'I can't stand no more of it, Bobs. Family not speaking, and everybody knowing about it.'

He said, 'No. Course you can't. Who done your head?'

I said, 'Usual place. Not Antoine though. He didn't want to do it. Said it'd break his heart. He got young Courtney to do it for me. It'll grow back.'

He said, 'Yeah. It'll grow back before you know it. And Roxy'll be chuffed. It was a shock, though. It's a very funny feeling, seeing you like that. Who's seen it?'

I said, 'Nobody. I haven't even looked at it myself. Not really. I come straight home in a scarf after I'd had it done, and I've been here on my Jack Jones. Has anybody seen you?'

He said, 'Nobody that knows me. It's called a makeover. They do them at that shop.'

It wasn't so much the clothes. He was wearing a navy and fuchsia two-piece with a little fuchsia vest top underneath. I'd seen him in that before. But they'd done his face and his hair. Eyeshadow and mascara and the works, and lipstick. Not just a little dab like I'd seen him do before. A proper mouth. And his shape was different.

I said, 'What's happened to your bum?'

He said, 'Padding. They're called Femmeform pads. Don't they make a difference? They're a bit hot, mind. You put them in these special knickers. And beard concealer. Did you notice that? It's like your Max Factor, only a bit thicker. Are you really divorcing me, Ba?'

I said, 'I don't know.' It just come out. I was that sure before he turned up, and then when he walked in it was nice to see him back. Even though.

I told him the latest on Roxy. He said, 'I should do what you did. Tell Jason straight and then just turn up at the hospital.' Then he saw what I was thinking. He said, 'No, not like this. Not *dressed*. I wouldn't do that. We could go together. How about this afternoon?'

I said, 'It'd mean taking all that stuff off.'

He said, 'Course.' And I thought it would be nice to have somebody with me, first time out with no hair.

I said, 'You shouldn't have gone to bed with all that muck on your face anyway. It's bad for your skin.' He smiled. First time in a long while I'd seen him do that.

He said, 'Ba, do you know, now I'm getting over the shock, you look really lovely with no hair. I never knowed you'd got such a lovely-shaped head.'

I suppose he was hoping I'd tell him how nice he

looked, but I couldn't do it. Too much make-up, and the wig was wrong as well. Too young, and too big. It was like Farrah Fawcett what's her name. Nobody does their hair like that any more. And here's another thing. All this matching shoes and handbag business. Women don't do that any more. Not real women. And it's definitely not right for him. My Bobs has always dressed smart but casual. I said, 'That skirt'd look better with some little flat pumps.'

Sister Galloway was on duty. I just stood in her office door till she looked up. She said, 'Oh, my word! Mrs Bradshaw! Look at you!' and she come and gave me a great big hug. She said Roxy had had a bad night. She said, 'We think she's got an infection. It happens sometimes. And the medicine's making her feel sick. That happens, too. It's just a little hiccup. But wait till she sees her new-look gran. She'll be tickled pink.'

I said, 'Is her dad with her?'

She said, 'He is. Her mum's gone home for a break. How are things?'

I said, 'He's here. He's waiting downstairs while I get the lie of the land.'

She hummed and hawed a bit when I told her that. I said, 'It's all right. He's got proper clothes on. It's just Jason we're worried about. We don't want a big scene, but it's breaking Bobs' heart not seeing her. And she keeps asking for him.'

She said, 'I know she does. But I don't want Roxy upset. I won't have any shouting on my ward.'

I went down to get Bobs, and she went to fetch Jason, to get him into the corridor, away from Roxy in case he blew up.

He said, 'Well, now I know you're round the bend' when he seen my head. Then he spotted his dad. He said, 'You've got some effing nerve.' Using a word like that in front of Sister Galloway.

Bobs said, 'Son, I'm not here for a scrap. I'm just asking you to reconsider. Say what you like about me, but I've been a good grandad. Haven't I been a good grandad? And I know Roxy keeps asking for me. Whatever must she think? She must be thinking her grandad don't love her no more.'

He was filling up and so was Jason.

He said, 'I'm begging you, son.'

Jason blowed his nose. He said, 'Five minutes.'

We'd got her a Pony World horse and foal set and the fully jointed rider, but she was too poorly to be bothered with it. We sat either side of her, and she just lay there, twiddling his hair with one hand and stroking my head with the other.

She said, 'It feels nice, Nana. It feels a bit tickly.' That was because it was growing back already. It's going to be nearly as much trouble as when I went platinum. And I shall have to keep it up because hers won't be growing back for a long while.

She said, 'Gemma's not got a grandad.' Gemma's her little friend at school. Every week they send her something. A big picture they've all drawn, or something. Anyway, she flung her arms round Bobs. She said, 'I'm glad you're my grandad, Grandad. I don't like it when you have to go away.'

I had a quick look to make sure Jason had heard that. He'd heard.

By the time we come away I'd almost forgot about my head. There were people looking at it and I just weren't bothered any more. Bobs gave me a squeeze in the lift. He said, 'You look like that Sigourney Weaver.'

Sigourney Weaver's big sister, more like.

He said, 'Well, that cleared the air a bit. Do you fancy calling in at the clubhouse?'

I said, 'Saturday? It'll be busy?'

He said, 'That's what I mean. Let everyone get an eyeful of your new hairdo. Give them something to talk about.'

Give them something *else* to talk about. It was all right for him, looking all normal in his blazer. I could just imagine Della Astley saying, 'Well, I heard he was having a sex change and she was divorcing him.'

And Valerie Palfreyman saying, 'By the looks of her head it must be the other way round. Who told you?'

He said, 'It's up to you.'

So we went, and I was that pleased when I spotted Mary's car.

I said, 'Mack's got a race in mind for Tiger Lil.'

He said, 'I know. I talked to him. But she's your horse. Yours and Mary's. Just listen to what Mack tells you. He knows what he's doing. We could drive down tomorrow, if you like, and have a look at her. Get a bit of lunch.' He kept talking as if nothing was wrong, like nothing had changed. I tell him I'm divorcing him and he says, 'How about a drive out?'

You could have heard a pin drop when we walked into that bar.

He said, 'Come on Ba, let's get the bull by the horns,' and he walked straight across to Mary. She was sitting with the Astleys and Phyllis Crawford. He said, 'All right, Mary? Ba's had all her hair off, to keep our Roxy company. Isn't she a marvel?' She coloured up, and she was giving me the old eyebrow routine, wanting to know what was going on.

He said, 'I hear Mack's got plans for Tiger Lil.'

I could see Phyllis Crawford fathoming out what to do. I could see her trying to remember if there was anything in the club rules about letting women in without their hair.

Mary said, 'Wolverhampton, or Newbury, I think that's what he said.'

'Newmarket,' Bobs said, 'Newmarket, not Newbury.'

Mary said, 'Well, I hope it's going to be Wolverhampton. That'd be nice and handy. And it might get in the *Evening News* as well. No sense in paying out for a horse if nobody round here knows you've got it.'

He said, 'No, Wolverhampton would just be some little graduation race. But if Mack enters her for Newmarket then we know we're really in business. Eh, Clive?'

Della Astley had never took her eyes off my head, but I'm not altogether sure Clive had noticed. He said, 'Will she go a mile?'

Bobs said, 'Remains to be seen. She's fast. Mack told me she's looking faster than City Index and she's just won a Group Two at Sandown in tough company.'

Della said, 'I'm going to the little girls' room,' and Phyllis said, 'Me too.'

So that got shot of them. Clive Astley got his diary out and wrote Tiger Lil's name down. He said, 'Always interesting to talk to connections. I shall watch out for her.'

Mary said, 'Well, I still think Wolverhampton

would be better. Douglas says you can sit at your lunch table and see the races, and they'll come and put your bets on for you and everything. Douglas says you can stay there all afternoon and never budge.'

Bobs said, 'Scouser all right? Haven't seen him in a week or two.'

She said, 'He's chocker with work. More work than he knows what to do with.'

Bobs said, 'Tell him to drop by. Have a beer on his way home one night. Or we could have a night out. Get dolled up and go to the Lombard Room.'

I seen her flinch when he said that.

'Or the Maharaja', he said. 'Have a nice night out. Get a mixed grill.'

I've never been able to decide if he were doing it on purpose, to wind her up, or if he just don't see things from anybody else's point of view.

When we come out of the clubhouse he said, 'You were quiet in there.'

I said, 'Everybody was looking at me.'

He said, 'Clive Astley weren't. Anyway, Ba, stuff 'em. What do you care about them for? They've all got bad perms and old-lady humps.'

I said, 'You know who else never batted an eye? The steward.'

He said, 'Ken? Yes, you're right. But we pay his

wages, don't forget. That's his job, being pleasant and serving you your drink.' Which is true.

He said, 'Anyway, he was in Aden. Must have seen all sorts out there.'

He said, 'I was wondering . . .'

We'd come back from seeing Roxy and going to the golf club, and we were just sitting in the kitchen like old times, only it wasn't old times and I'd got my bed made up in Mel's old room.

He said, 'There's a little get-together next Saturday. Up in Warley. Just in somebody's house. And the wives go. I was just wondering . . .'

I'd been feeling really great, because Jason and his dad were speaking again, and everybody thought I'd done a good thing getting my head shaved. And then he had to go and spoil it.

He said, 'It's just ordinary people, Ba. Like you and me. It's just a little club where the men can dress and the wives can come along. We could just go for half an hour.'

I said, 'Is there no end to this?' And he said, 'No, sweetheart. I don't think there is.'

I went into town on Saturday afternoon. I bought a nice big stetson for weekends and an ordinary felt hat with a little feather on the side, in case I have to go anywhere awkward. It's not that I mind people looking. I've got used to it now. But it's turned chilly this last week.

He picked me up outside Safeway, and if it hadn't been for his BOB 500 number plate, I wouldn't have been sure it was him. He was in a jade wool jacket and a new white blouse with ruffles. It was a lovely jacket. He said, 'Now, it's Stephanie and Peggy's house we're going to. Stephanie's a surveyor, big land surveys, drains and motorways and stuff like that, all computerized. Got exams and everything. He's been dressing for years. And Peggy does something. I think she's a teacher.'

I said, 'Stephanie's the man?'

He said, 'Yes?' Like it was obvious.

I said, 'What's his real name?'

He said, 'I don't know, Nobody needs to know that. That's the whole point of something like Buttons and Bows. You can just go there dressed *femme* and nobody thinks anything of it. Stephanie is Stephanie.'

Dressed *femme*. I had to think about that for a minute. It's French.

I said, 'And how come you know him?'

He said, 'The shop I go to. They have a noticeboard. Clubs and get-togethers. There's always something. Don't matter who you are or where you live, there's always somebody you can meet. And there's phone numbers. Counselling. Anything you care to mention.'

So we were crawling up the M5, keeping it just under seventy because he was wearing a frilly blouse and a rope of pearls and he didn't want to get pulled over, and it suddenly dawned on me.

I said, 'So if he's Stephanie, who are you?'

He said, 'Bebe.'

I said, 'What kind of a name is that?'

He said, 'You know? "Welcome to Life with the Lyons, starring Ben Lyon and Bebe Daniels." '

I said, 'Couldn't you have picked something better than that? How about Roberta?'

He said, 'Oh, no. I wouldn't like that. Remember Roberta Hendry?'

We were at school with her. She had legs like tree trunks and I think she joined the WRAF.

I said, 'Or Bobbie? That can be a woman's name.'

Sometimes I can't believe what's happened to my life. Sitting there with no hair and my husband wearing a skirt, on my way to some little house in Warley. We've got two businesses and planning permission for a swimming pool. We've got a daughter married to a Godbold, and Bobs is in the Elks. Used to be.

He said, 'No. It's Bebe. B B. Get it? Bobs Bradshaw. Be Be.'

There was a parking space right outside, thank God, and there was another couple getting out of a car on the bit of land running up the side of the house. A big redhead, looked as if she could hardly get behind the steering wheel, and a little skinny husband in puffed sleeves and a bow tied round the back. Looked like little Bo-Beep with a shaving shadow.

Bobs waved to them. He said, 'That's Jill. And his wife's Carole.'

I said, 'How many times have you been here?' But I never got an answer to that because Peggy was at the door kissing everybody and carrying on.

She said, 'Barbara, welcome to our little circle. Come and give me a hand with the sandwiches.'

It reminded me of our kitchen when I lived at home. The old cabinet with the drop-down front, and the Ascot over the sink. You forget people live like that. I mean, we had Smallbones in and they done everything. Chopping boards set in the worktop, little swing-out carousels in the corner cupboards, waste disposable. Everything.

She said, 'Now, Barbara, just make yourself at home. They're a nice crowd, and we're all in the same boat, you know. All in the same boat, so nobody has to explain themselves to anybody. Do you think I've done enough food?'

I said, 'How many are you expecting?'

'Could be eight' she said, 'could be twelve. You never know. How's your little granddaughter?'

See? People know all your business.

There was eight of us in the end. Georgette and Rosemary didn't turn up till quite a bit later, and he was done up like a dog's breakfast. Ankle-strap sandals and a wig like blummin' Cher. They'd just come back from Majorca. Apparently there's this hotel that turns a blind eye. Carole and her husband go to one in Benidorm, she was telling me.

She said, 'How did it go then, Rosemary? You're not very brown.'

Rosemary said, 'I hardly went out. He did. Didn't you? Sunbathing all day and clubbing every night. I stayed put, though. I took a bag full of murders with me and stayed put.'

Peggy said, 'Yes, well, you don't always want to go out and face people, do you?'

Rosemary said, 'No, it's not that. I don't like the sun. I wanted to go to Norway.'

Bobs and the others, Jill and Stephanie and Georgette, they were just talking about the cricket and car engines and stuff like that. Peggy had done egg-and-cress sandwiches, ham-and-pickle, and sponge cake. She went to make a fresh pot of tea, and I was going to follow her out to the kitchen, just for a breather, but Carole, the big one, said, 'Barbara, would you mind ever so much if I had a little feel of your head?'

She said, 'Oh, it's growing back. It's like peach.' So then they all wanted a feel.

She said to me, 'You've got some guts, to do a thing like that.' But I haven't. It's our Roxy that's got the guts.

When we were leaving Carole said to me, 'It's at our house next time. I hope we shall see the pair of you.'

Peggy said, 'We take turns.'

Oh no they don't. Not in Alvechurch.

Monday afternoon Scouser turned up. I were out the back, planting daffs, and he come up behind me and just stood there. I nearly jumped out of my blummin' skin.

I said, 'Hello, stranger.'

He said, 'I know, I know. I just didn't know what to do for the best, Ba. When Mary told me, I wanted to come straight round. But then I thought, Best to leave it a bit. Let the dust settle. I like your head. You look like that Sinead O'Connor.'

I've thought for quite a while he needed his eyes testing.

He said, 'Anyway, here I am. And I'm that thrilled.'

I said, 'How do you mean?'

He said, 'That you've come to your senses. It's been a long wait, but it'll be worthwhile.'

I said, 'Scouser, are you talking about what I think you're talking about?'

He said, 'You and me. After you've divorced him. I got you, babe!'

I said, 'Mary knows about this, does she? About you running off with me?'

He said, 'Well . . .'

I said, 'Because she never mentioned it when we were having a drink with her down the club house. You'd think she would have done.'

He said, 'Any chance of a tea?'

We went inside and I told him. I said, 'First off, I don't know if I am divorcing him, but, if I do, I shan't be going anywhere with you, Vickery. Not with you and not with anybody else. If I can't have my Bobs I shall just be a gran and do my garden. But if you're miserable with Mary, leave her. Just don't involve me. Are you miserable? You always look all right to me.'

He said, 'We've never been like you and Bradshaw.'

I said, 'Right, now let's talk about him, since you brought his name up. Why haven't you been to see him? How come you've never phoned him?'

He said, 'I don't know. What am I supposed to say to him? "Bring your lipsticks round for swaps"?'

I said, 'It's not funny, Scouser.' But actually it is quite funny. I was just thinking about Stephanie at the club, with his great big Adam's apple, and

Georgette with his size 12 stilettos, and Scouser just caught me on my funny bone. He was dunking Hobnobs and we were laughing that much he dropped half one in his tea.

He said, 'How's Roxy and the bab?'

I told him. She's got another fortnight on this medicine that makes her feel so poorly, and after that she has to have X-rays. They have to make sure it hasn't spread. Blair's all right. I never hardly see him. I think Scouser was quite taken with him, though. It's a pity him and Mary never had more kids. Family can keep you going really, when you feel like jacking it all in.

I said, 'So will you phone him? Have a drink with him?'

He said, 'Yeah. I will. I seen a UFO, did I tell you? Driving back from Bewdley, about a week ago. I spotted these lights in the sky, quite low and following me, so I stopped and wound the window down, and they stopped. So then I drove a bit further, stopped again, and they stopped. So then I got out.'

I said, 'Get away! You wouldn't even get out of bed and look when you had that owl sitting on your balcony making funny noises. Mary told me.'

'No,' he said, 'it weren't like that. I felt completely calm. I thought, Well, if they'd come for me there was nothing I could do about it. Just try to remember everything so I could sell my story to the *Mail*, if I ever got back.'

I said, 'So what happened?'

He said, 'Ruddy transit van come tooting past me, banging on his horn because I'd forgot to put my blinkers on. Must have frightened them off.'

I said, 'Where did they go?'

He said, 'That's the thing about them, Ba. One minute they're there, next minute they're gone. And you never hear a thing. Now, Les Timmins, remember Les Timmins? He lost time. He was driving along somewhere, up Market Drayton way, bright lights in the sky, electrics went dead, and when he come to he'd lost two hours. He told the police, but, of course, nothing ever come of it. It all got hushed up. There's government cover-ups. And he reckons he's never felt the same since. Lost time, they call it.'

Lost time. Les Timmins has been losing time since the first day he ever walked into a pub.

He said, 'So if I was to meet him for a beer, one night this week, say, would he . . . you know . . . would he have his stuff on?'

I said, 'Good heavens, no. He only does it in front of me, and at this club he goes to.'

If he started wanting to go out, if he started flaunting himself, that would be the end.

Tiger Lil's running next week in the Dewhurst Stakes and our Roxy's getting on really well. Her bone marrow's clear and she's holding up all right with these rays they're giving her in her brain. Bald as a coot, but that don't bother her no more. Now she's out of bed she takes me all round, when I go to visit, showing off her nana that's got no hair. The only problem with going racing is things have been a bit chilly between me and Mary since all this business with Bobs come out. You can understand it, the way people talk.

Scouser's over the worst of it now. He come round one night, looking a bit sheepish, and they talked shop, just like old times, and then he said, 'Are you going to put your stuff on then, Bradshaw? Let's have a gander. I've heard enough about it.'

Then it were Bobs' turn to look embarrassed. He said, 'Do you mean it? No. You'll laugh.'

Scouser said, 'Too bloody right I'll laugh, but you must be getting used to that.'

Bobs said, 'What should I put on, Ba? What do you think?'

Now this is the thing. He's got more clothes now than Typhoo have got tea leaves, and some of it's boring old stuff – pleated skirts, cardigans – and then he's got a couple of things split up to here and plunging down to there, make him look like Danny La Rue. I was talking to Carole about it, because her husband always dresses the same way: little floral prints, shirtwaisters, plain courts with a medium heel. She said to me, 'Bebe's still finding his style. Everybody's different. Now, Naomi, you've never met him because he's moved to Cornwall, but he used to come to the socials in a jumper and slacks, and I used to think, well *that's* not cross-dressing, but then I found out they were ladies' jumpers and slacks he was wearing. He knew they were ladies' wear, you see, and that was good enough for him. Now, Georgette, he just wants to look like a tart. Whereas my Jill likes to look nice. A lot of them do. And I think Bebe might be the same. He's still experimenting, but I've got a feeling he'll end up more like my Jill.'

I thought, 'I blummin' hope not.' He reminds me of that school we sent Melody to when she was nine.

All them mothers in their Laura Ashley skirts and their Alice bands.

Anyway, he disappeared upstairs and he was gone ages. Scouser said to me, 'Is this it then? Are you sticking with him?'

I said, 'For the time being. Anyway, I've told you. I'm not interested.'

He said, 'I wonder how things would have worked out? You know, if it'd been me and you together right from the start?'

I said, 'Why don't you and Mary go to America and see your Fleur? How long is it since you've seen her?'

He said, 'Yeah, we'll probably go for Christmas.'

But they won't. They always say they will, but they never do.

He said, 'It's Fleur and Mary. You know? Five minutes and they're rowing.'

Same as me and Melody. But family's family. You don't not see family at Christmas just because you don't get on.

I must say, when Bobs eventually come down he did look nice. He was wearing that ivory skirt with the flowers on it, with a long-sleeved jersey top and a plaited leather belt. I know he's got a hankering for a little sleeveless dress and a pillbox hat like Jackie O. He's always loved her; ever since she was Mrs Kennedy.

But he does look better with his arms covered. They all do.

Scouser said, 'Well I'll be jiggered.'

Bobs had toned everything down for Scouser. Just a bit of lipstick and his little silver clip-ons.

Scouser said, 'I've never seen nothing like it. I thought you'd be in sequins and them big sexy high heels. I didn't think you'd look like a real woman.'

Course, Bobs' face lit up when he heard that. He said, 'So what do you think?'

Scouser said, 'Amazing. I could have walked past you in the street. If you wasn't so tall and you hadn't got such big hands, I could have walked past you in the street and never looked twice. Incredible.'

Bobs relaxed after that. I've noticed that. When he dresses he always looks on edge for the first few minutes, and then it's like he forgets. And I'm getting that I forget sometimes as well. Just for a minute or two. Even though it's my Bobs' voice I can hear, it don't seem that peculiar any more. He does make a nice woman. He even sits nice. When I think what he's like, sitting in front of the telly in his jeans, legs akimbo, taking up all the settee, scratching and trumping and carrying on, and then I see him in a skirt, behaving himself, I can't believe it's the same man.

When he was going Scouser said, 'When we see you next week, when we go to Newmarket, I think it'd be best if Mary didn't know. About tonight and Bobs putting his dress on? She's still a bit funny about it. So I'll just tell her everything's sorted out and everybody's pals, and everything. All right? And if Tiger Lil wins she'll be putty in my hands. If we get into that Winner's Enclosure, she'll be offering you the run of her wardrobe.'

Bobs said, 'We'd all better pray for overnight rain then.'

Scouser was just driving off. He leaned out the window and he shouted, 'Oi, Bradshaw, you could do with a Ladyshave round them legs.'

I had intended going just as I was. Getting Courtney to do my head again a few days before and not bothering with a hat. But I heard these women in Rackham's coffee shop. One of them said, 'Look at that woman. She looks like a Martian.' The other one said, 'She must have cancer. You'd think they'd have given her a wig. Fancy walking round looking like that. It's putting me off my gâteau.' And I was worried about Mary anyway. She can really put a crimp in your day if she's not happy, and I did want us all to have a nice day out, just like old times. So I fished out a scarf with horseshoes and stuff on it, and practised tying it round my head like a turban.

Melody come round one lunchtime. She said, 'Well are you getting divorced, or what?'

I said, 'We're trying to work things out. How's married life treating you?'

She said, 'It's dead boring. He's always got work to do. Every night. Papers, papers.'

I said, 'Well, that's how it is when you're your own boss.'

She said, 'Dad never brought work home.'

I said, 'You don't remember. Not papers, maybe, but he brought it home inside his head. Still does. It'd be nice for him to see his daughter once in a while as well. It'd be nice for him to get asked round for dinner one fine day.'

She said, 'Well, I can't hardly do that if he's turning into a pervert and you're divorcing him, can I? I've got Andrew to think of.'

I said, 'Well, he's not, and I'm not, so there's nothing stopping you now. What does Andrew think about it?'

I already knowed the answer to that because I'd bumped into his dad in Bromsgrove and he'd said to me, 'Hold your head high, my dear. Every family's got its secrets and there are plenty worse than yours. And I know I speak for Audrey, too, and Andrew.'

She said, 'I don't know. I'm not talking to him about that. The Godbolds don't believe in divorce. I know that much.'

Funny attitude for solicitors. I think it must just be Godbold divorces they don't believe in.

Come the day, it was that cold and damp, Bobs said to me, 'Put your thermals on, Ba. That Newmarket wind is like a knife through butter.' So I put my old furry favourite on, pulled it down low over my eyebrows, and he started whistling 'Lara's Theme'. He always did like Julie Christie.

I was for going on the train because I didn't fancy being cooped up in the car with Mary on that long drive. I know we're all supposed to be good pals again, but there was still a bit of an atmosphere, and at least on a train you can get up and go for a little walk. I said to Bobs, 'We could all have a drink, as well. We wouldn't have to worry about getting breathalysed.'

He said, 'I don't mind driving. You know that. Drinking don't bother me.'

Scouser agreed with me and Mary agreed with Bobs. So we ended up driving.

It weren't properly light when we set off, and I had to sit in the back with Mary because Scouser had got the *Racing Post* and Bobs wanted him to read it out to him, see if it said anything different to the *Sporting Life*.

They've got a wedding to go to, Mary and Scouser. Mary's sister's boy. She said, 'Whatever are you supposed to wear in November? I don't know why they can't wait till the spring. Give people a chance to wear a nice hat.'

Everybody knows why they can't wait till the spring. It's common knowledge.

I said, 'What about something furry, like this one?'

She said, 'Oh, no. Fur stinks.'

I said, 'Any sign of Fleur coming over for Christmas?'

Fleur's been engaged to this Pete, must be three years now, and they never fly over or seem to get any nearer to naming the day. And Scouser and Mary don't go there. Hardly ever. If one of ours had emigrated we'd be visiting all the time. Not that ours would emigrate.

She said, 'No. They don't really bother with Christmas in America. They have Thanksgiving.'

We've been to America. They have shops that sell Christmas trimmings all year round. Still, I didn't want an argument with her. I wanted us all to have a nice day out.

The *Sporting Life* said Tiger Lil would be experiencing a huge rise in class. And the *Racing Post* said Designer Label was the one they all had to beat.

We'd got a table booked in the Members', but after we'd had our seafood mousse Bobs went looking for Mack, and he was gone so long we had our loin of pork without him. The waitress said it didn't matter. She said he could have it any time. That's the difference, you see, when you're an owner you get better service all round.

I said, 'What kept you?'

He said, 'I walked a bit of the course with Mack, and it's drying out fast, so that's not so good. We want rain. We want it to start now and not stop till three o'clock.'

Mary said, 'You've got something on your chin.'

Grease. The waitress come to see if he was ready for his roast, but he said, 'No, thanks love, I've just had a steak sandwich and double onions down in the Silver Ring. What's the pudding situation?'

He was kidding her about bringing him extra ice cream with his apple tart, seeing as how he hadn't had his main course, and she got a bit flustered. I mean, she knowed he was somebody because Mary had told her we'd got a horse running, so she didn't want to cross him, but on the other hand, I suppose they do have their rules. Actually, I think she fancied him. Women do fancy my Bobs and he does look smashing in his Aquascruton coat.

It didn't rain. I had Granny's Pet in the 2.05 and Galapino in the 2.35, both come in second, so that weren't a very good omen. There wasn't a cloud in the sky and it was cold enough to freeze hell. We went down to the parade ring, and there was a big crowd of Pakistanis in shiny suits. Scouser reckoned they was Arab royalty, but Scouser would. We went to York one time for the Magnet Cup and he swore the Duke of Kent had stood next to him in the Gents, but Bobs had been in there at the same time and he hadn't noticed him.

Designer Label was favourite, but there was late money for Leylat Jameel, and Tiger Lil had come in from 25/1 to 14/1. Bobs said it was because she was walking so nice in the ring. Funny, they all look the same to me. Just horses going round and round with their blankets on. She was bigger than I remembered though, and livelier looking as well.

Des Fogarty was riding for us again.

Scouser said, 'What's our chances, do you reckon?'

Des said, 'I rode her work last week, sir, and she's come on lovely since the summer. She's got a lot of kick in her for a filly.'

Mary said, 'Don't stand so near to her then, Douglas.'

We waited till they began to go down to the start and then we went across to the grandstand. I was that nervous I needed the lav again, but I daren't go in case I missed anything. Bobs stood behind me with his arms wrapped round me to keep me warm. I love it when he does that.

They were all at the start except for Pattypan, and she was going down like she'd got all day. Mary said, 'Well that one doesn't look much cop,' but Bobs explained to her how you sometimes have to be gentle and take your time, to stop a horse boiling over before the race has even started.

Scouser was watching the monitor. He said, 'There's something up. Des has dismounted,' and for a minute we all thought the worst. Then they announced it. 'Number four has unseated her rider, but he seems none the worse for it. Number six has just arrived at the start and gone behind the stalls, so they'll be starting to load them.'

Mary kept whispering, 'Come on Tiger Lil, come on Tiger Lil,' and they weren't even running. Then they were off. Leylat Jameel was first to break, and the rest of them stayed in a bunch for two, nearly three furlongs. They were all going like the clappers, apart from Pattypan, and she was tailed off. Designer Label was on the rail. Then Lissarulla Lass moved across next to Mumkin, and she was boxed in. That left our baby with nothing but fresh air in front of her, apart from Leylat Jameel, and she was yards clear. I heard Scouser say, 'He's left it too late', and Designer Label had gone wide and was starting to make tracks. But she hadn't got the beating of our little star, and when they hit the rise, just before the finish, there was only Leylat Jameel fighting to hold on, and the rest of them were all in a heap. Tiger Lil from Leylat Jameel by a head, and Designer Label was third.

I've never known anything like it. Mary was kissing me, and Scouser and Bobs and Mack. Them Pakis in the shiny suits could have been kissing me for all I cared.

Mack said, 'Blistering race. Let's see what Des has to say.'

And Bobs said, 'Get down to that Winner's Enclosure, woman, and make yourself useful for a change.'

Course, you don't get the money straight off. It's not like the Lottery. There was some to go to Mack, and some to Des Fogarty. But I got presented with a little silver dish, and Des got champagne. I took Mary up with me. It was my turn, but we are joint owners, and the telly people were there and I didn't want her sulking all the way home.

Des had to scoot off because he was in the next race, but he said, 'She was a bit of a hooligan, down at the start. I don't think we've got to the bottom of this one yet, Ma'am.' And Mack said, 'She's fast. We'll see how she winters, but I think we should go for the Guineas.'

I've seen some men with silly smiles on their faces in my time, but I've never seen anything as soft-looking as Scouser and Bobs when Mack said that.

Mary said to me, 'That's good, is it? The Guineas?'

It was getting foggy, so we didn't stop till Corley Services, and then we heard there'd been a big smash on the M42 and everything was backed up, so Bobs said, 'I'll carry on into town. What's it to be? A curry or a curry?'

So we went to the Maharaja, because we like it there. Bhupinder always remembers us. Always looks after us. Anyway, who should be sat in there but Jill and Carole from the whassisname club.

Course, they spotted me because of my hair, and they waved hello, and I could see them looking and looking at Bobs. I don't suppose they'd ever seen him in proper clothes.

Mary and Scouser hadn't noticed nothing. It was that busy there we were lucky to get a table. Bobs says to Bhupinder, 'You must need a surgical truss. All the lolly you have to carry home at night.' He laughed.

So we had poppadoms all round, I had the king prawn bhuna with onion kulcha, Mary and Bobs had the tandoori mixed grill, and they done Scouser an omelette and chips because he had a bad do once with a vindaloo in Kingswinford, and he's been wary ever since.

Once we'd ordered, Mary's eyes started swivelling, to see if there was anybody in she recognized. All of a sudden she said, 'Don't look now, but one of them women over there isn't. Look how he's sitting.' And it is a funny thing because Jill's only a skinny little specimen. He must only wear a size 10. But he sits like a navvy, whereas my Bobs, who's built like a brick outhouse, when he's got his stuff on, he sits like a real lady.

Then she caught me and Bobs looking at each other, and she remembered. She said, 'Oh, my giddy aunt. It's everywhere. The world's gone mad. Don't say anything. I don't want to know about it. We've had a lovely day and I don't want it spoiled. Now am I right in thinking that if Tiger Lil runs in this Guineas, it'll be my turn to go up and have my photo taken? If she wins?'

Bobs said, 'Well, Mack'll probably give her another run before that. He'll probably find a race for her round about the middle of April, so we can see how she's fared over the winter.'

She had a think about that. She said, 'This Guineas, it's a famous race, isn't it?'

I said, 'Very famous. And I'll tell you what I think, Mary. I think, if Tiger Lil wins we should both be in the photo, and never mind whose turn it is.'

Scouser said, 'Which one of them's the man did you say?' He weren't even looking in the right direction.

Mary said, 'Douglas! We're not discussing that. We've already agreed.'

We were just running the Dewhurst again, for about the hundredth time and Carole and Jill were getting their coats. Bobs said, 'Come and have a drink with us before you go. We're celebrating.'

They come across to our table. Mary's eyes were sticking out like organ stops and Scouser were catching flies in his mouth. They said they wouldn't stop. They had to get back for the babysitter. Everybody just said, 'Nice to meet you,' and Mary managed a smile.

After they'd gone Scouser said, 'Bad wig.'

He was right. Jill's got one of them dark-brown page-boys with a big thick fringe, and he's got heavy eyebrows. He'd be better off with something wispy.

On the way home, just before we dropped them off, Mary said, 'I was just thinking about the photos. If Tiger Lil wins, do you think your hair'll be growed back by then, Ba?'

This treatment Roxy's having now; it's the worst bit so far. The X-rays aren't so bad because she just has to lie there, but she's having injections as well. She has to curl up in a ball and they go in through a gap in her backbone. She's got a mouth full of ulcers as well. Sister Galloway said it's the drugs. So we took her a Jurassic Park Dino Gulper and a Sip-O-Saurus Crazy Straw to try to get her drinking more, and story tapes for her to listen to on her headphones.

She said, 'Are we coming to your house for Christmas?'

Christmas. I hadn't even thought about it.

Diane said, 'We'll be stopping at home this year. It'll be easier. My mum's flying over.'

I don't know where that leaves us. We've always had them at our house on Christmas Day. Last year Jason and Diane were invited to a party on Christmas

Eve, so they brought the kiddies over to us and put them to bed. I don't know who was the most excited, Roxy or Bobs. He got me to stand out on the landing while he was tucking her up, shaking a cat's collar to sound like blummin' sleigh-bells. We've always had the monkey puzzle lit up in the front garden and two big trees indoors, one in the hall done all in silver and one in the lounge for the kiddies, every colour of the rainbow and little chocolate things hanging.

I said, 'Well, you'll have to be at your house this year. See your other nana.'

She said, 'But Santa always comes to your house.'

Bobs said, 'Don't you worry. I'll make sure he knows. I've got to have a word with him anyway. What's he supposed to be bringing you?'

She said, 'A bike. Blair's getting Premium Bonds because he's only a baby. I know, New Zealand Nana could come with us to your house.'

I said, 'Whatever your mummy decides. We'll see you. Don't you worry.'

Diane sat there and she never said a word.

When we got outside he said, 'You drive.' He was on the mobile dialling Jason. I said, 'Leave it, Bobs. If they're not coming to us and they don't want us there, we'll make our own arrangements.'

He said, 'I just want to hear him say it. I just want him to come out with it and say we're not seeing them for Christmas.' But Jason weren't there. He just got the machine. So by the time we got home he was in a right old paddy. First thing he done when we got in was pour a drink. Second thing he done was go and put a blouse and skirt on.

I'm not that bothered. If Jason's going to take that attitude, I'd sooner stop away.

He got through later on. Jason said how you can't expect things to be the same every year, which is true, and how they'd maybe pop over on Boxing Day, which was fair enough, and Roxy'd be easily tired this year, so they didn't want a load of excitement, which was fair enough as well, but Bobs was determined to have a row. In the end I grabbed the phone off him and said to Jason, 'What your dad means is, of course we hope we'll see the kiddies at Christmas, and we'll fit in with whatever you decide.'

I said, 'That was clever. Antagonizing him. I've only just got you back on speaking terms.'

He said, 'He's playing games with us. Now he's got this on me, he's going to keep using it and using it.'

I said, 'Yeah. Never mind they might want Christmas in their own place. Never mind Roxy's been at death's door, and her other nan's flying all the way from New Zealand. This has all got to be about you. Is that how it's going to be now? Every time somebody thwarts you it's going to be because you wear dresses? Discrimination, is that it? You'll be going on marches next. You'll be wanting compensation.'

He said, 'I'm still not allowed to see Blair. Don't tell me that's not what it's about when I'm still not allowed to see my grandson. They think it's catching. That's what it is.'

I said, 'Oh, put a sock in it. Nobody's even thinking about that any more. And we don't have to stay here, hanging about till they say we can visit. We can go away. Clear off to Lanzarote.'

Blummin' men. They put a pair of tights on and a bit of lipstick and they think the world's going to stop turning.

The Christmas social was at Jill and Carole's house, out Acock's Green way. Stephanie and Peggy were there, but I didn't know anybody else. There was Cynthia and Jenny, and Arlene and Michelle, only I got them the wrong way round. It was *him* that was Arlene and her that was Michelle. And there was an older couple that had never been before, Vicky and Doris, and Vicky was wearing this embroidered see-through top, kingfisher chiffon with jet beads over a little camisole and short skirt, and H-bar sandals. And too much blusher. Ridiculous. He hadn't even got good legs. I mean, when you get to sixty and you've got veins like bunches of grapes, you don't wear a skirt half way up your BTM. You'd think his wife would have said something. I would.

Anyway, it was all very nice. Carole had made

lasagne, and Jill had done mince pies, and everybody had took something, a party pack or a tin of Pringles or something.

Carole said, 'Fancy us bumping into you in the Indian. We wouldn't have known you, if it hadn't been for your hair. We'd only ever seen Bebe dressed *femme*.'

I said, 'We'd been racing. We'd been out for the day with friends.'

She said, 'He doesn't go out dressed, then? Not as a general rule?'

Doris was standing against the wall, holding onto an empty glass.

I said, 'What are you drinking?'

She said, 'My husband doesn't go out dressed either.' Whispered it, she did.

I said, 'No? Well some of them do and some of them don't. It's a funny business, isn't it?'

She said, 'Which one's yours?'

I pointed him out.

I said, 'How long has yours been doing it?

She said, 'Thirty-seven years.'

Thirty-seven years. And he's still going round looking like Widow Twankey. I suppose it's like everything else in life. Some people just never learn.

She said, 'How about yours?'

I said, 'Six months, that I know of. You must

have known from the start, then?'

She said, 'Oh, yes. He told me before we got engaged. I've always known.'

Carole come and topped her glass up. She said, 'Have you had something to eat, Doris? Just help yourself. It's every man for himself here, if you know what I mean? Barbara's pretty new to us as well, aren't you? Ask Barbara. She'll tell you we don't bite.'

I asked her about family, but they'd never had any, and I asked her about work, but she'd been on the sick for years with her nerves. She said they'd got a cat, and she does a lot of them word puzzles, but that's not a life. When I think back on all the things you have to do when you've got a family, how you're on the go from early morning and there's always something needs seeing to, and I look at people who've never had kiddies, I wonder what they've done with all that time. They could have taken a blummin' slow boat to China just in the time I spent sewing name-tapes in Jason and Mel's kit.

She said, 'You've got some gumption. Coming out with no hair. Coming out to Christmas parties.' I said, 'Hair's nothing. Our little Roxy's in a ward full of kiddies with no hair. And I only come here because if he's out on a Saturday night I want to be out with him. I'm not here because I'm happy about it.'

I felt sorry for her, in a way, because some people just can't have kiddies, and that must be a terrible thing, but she was quite an annoying woman really. Full of troubles and every one of them a big long saga.

She said, 'We're in a council flat. We could get chucked out.'

Carole said, 'Course you couldn't. My sister's in a council place and she's had neighbours fighting with knives and keeping dogs chained up, barking day and night, and some of them have gentleman clients looking for business at all hours, and the council have never done a thing. Druggies and rowdies all over her estate, and men piddling in the lifts, and nobody ever gets chucked out, so don't you worry about that.'

Doris said, 'I don't sleep well either. Sleeping tablets don't touch me. Sometimes I wonder if it's worth carrying on.'

It was probably the wrong thing, to be sharp with someone who thinks they've got bad nerves, but I can't stand it when people won't help theirselves. I said, 'You want to get out and stop feeling so sorry for yourself. Get a little job, or do some voluntary. Things never seem so bad if you keep busy.'

She said, 'Oh, I couldn't do that. I get panic attacks. I've been under Dr Brynmor Jones for years.'

I wish now I hadn't done it, but it just come blurting out. I said, 'You want to pull yourself together. Seeing doctors for years if they're not doing you any good. You want to buck up and count your blessings.'

Then the waterworks started. Carole said, 'Oh Doris, Barbara didn't mean that how it sounded.' But I did. I've got no patience with anybody any more.

They were all looking at me, but I weren't bothered. Everybody's got something these days. Everybody's got syndromes. Messing around with doctors because the dark mornings get them down, or their kiddies won't sit still and learn anything at school. The blummin' strap. That was what made us sit still and learn. Everybody's just got excuses these days. And allergies. I don't know where they've all sprung from. I don't think they even knew about hayfever when we were kids.

Carole said, 'It is hard, the first few times you come out. We've all been through it. But it does get easier.'

Doris was standing there, trying not to cry any more. She'd took a mince pie to please Carole, but she was holding it like it was a hand grenade. She said, 'But it was our secret.'

And then I did feel for her. I touched her shoulder, and I weren't just doing it because Carole was giving

me the big signal. I really did feel for her, because
when your secret's out, it's like that bad dream, where
you're in Asda without a stitch on and everything
you try to hide behind is too small. I said, 'I'm sorry,
Doris', and that set her off again. She said, 'No. I
wish I could be like you.'

Vicky noticed her crying then, and he come over,
lipstick on his teeth. He said, 'What's up, lover?' But
she couldn't answer him.

Michelle and Peggy made her a cup of coffee, and
Carole fetched a box of Kleenex, and then Bobs,
Stephanie and Jill done us a Christmas medley. *Frosty
the Snowman, White Christmas, Deck Your Balls* and *I
Seen Mommy Kissing Santa Claus*, all lined up, doing
the harmony and everything. They ought to go on
the telly. They ought to go on *Stars In Their Eyes* as
the Beverley Sisters.

I was telling Bobs about Doris on the way home.
I said, 'All them years. But it was people knowing
she minded about. And with Carole and Jill, it's how
he looks she minds about. Whether he looks dainty.'

He said, 'And how about you? What do you mind
about?'

I said, 'I mind about you dressing up nice in an
appliqué blouse and then trumping like a trooper in
my car.'

Roxy's home for Christmas and Blair's walking. We dropped by on the way to the airport. Diane's mum was there. Betty. First time we'd seen her since Roxy's christening. She emigrated after Diane and Jason got married. She'd got a sister in Dunedin and she said people were nicer out there.

Course, Roxy was all over us, 'Come and see this, Grandad. Come and see my Advent calendar, Nanny.' And Blair was holding on to Bobs, steadying himself, because he's still a bit wobbly. That was when I knowed they'd said something to Betty. She was looking at Bobs like he was a bad smell, and then she started coaxing Blair, trying to get him away from his grandad. 'Blair, come to Nana Betty. Come and see the dicky birds.' And the more she called him the harder he hung on. He'd got his head buried in Bobs' trouser leg, laughing and clinging on, but Betty come and prised him off, pulling on his little fingers, and then he started crying.

Bobs said, 'Now then Barnacle Bill, it's your Nana Betty's turn for a cuddle. She don't get to see you as much as we do,' and he slipped Betty a chocolate snowman to give Blair. I could tell he was upset, though.

Roxy come and sat on my lap. We must have looked like a pair of electric light bulbs.

She said, 'Where are you going?'

I said, 'We're going to Tenerife for a bit of sunshine because your grandad's been working that hard, but don't you worry about your parcels. We've had a word with Father Christmas.'

We'd got them both clothes. They've got enough toys. A red zip-up snowsuit for Blair, and a coat with a velour collar and buttons and a matching hat for Roxy. Bobs had picked them out.

Roxy said, 'Who's going to look after Aunty Melody on Christmas time, then?'

I said, 'Aunty Mel's grown up. She looks after herself.' And don't she ever. I know they're going to the Godbolds for Christmas Day, and I know they're hoping to get a bit of wallpapering done, but she's never once asked us what we're doing. Never had us round for a drink, nor a bite to eat.

We'd had a card from the Godbolds, and a calendar

with scenes of Scotland, but I couldn't be bothered this year. Bobs said, 'Don't be like that, Ba,' so I said, 'Here's a biro, and you know where Smith's is. If you want to send cards you'd better get a move on.' We'd had them from all the Buttons and Bows crowd as well. And Pat and Gus, of course, with three doggy paw marks. It said *Love from Bruno, Tyson and their new little friend Sugar Ray*.

I don't know, though. I just wasn't in the mood. It's for kiddies, Christmas. If you haven't got kiddies you might as well clear off somewhere warm and save on your heating.

So we got this late booking for Puerto de la Cruz; four-star hotel, flight from Birmingham, and a Christmas dinner – £500, thank you very much, and that included a little Renault, in case we wanted to get to the golf course or anything. I phoned Mary from the travel agents because I could have got four places, but she said they were hanging on, waiting to hear if Fleur had managed to get a flight home, which, of course, she never did. I don't think she even tried.

It's a pity they didn't come because they would have loved it, and it would have kept Bobs on the straight and narrow, instead of me being on pins all the time in case he decided to go walkabout in one of his rigs. Thirty years we've been married and I've always done the packing. He's always told me what he wants to take, and then I pack it because men don't know how to fold. Anyway, this time I went up to do it and it was already done. So, of course, I smelled a rat, had a little look, and there was two skirts, two tops, and them sandals he likes so much.

He said, 'Just to wear in our room, Ba. Just to relax in.' And I was too tired to argue. Besides, everything was booked and I was looking forward to it. But the minute I knew that stuff was in his case, I knew I'd have to watch him. Give him an inch and he'll take a mile, my Bobs.

They all come out to wave us off, and I said to Betty, 'Well, have a lovely Christmas. Couldn't be much better, could it? Seeing Roxy home and doing so great.'

She said, 'I've been praying for her. Best thing for all of them would be to come back with me. Have a fresh start. Lovely clean air. That's what children need.'

It's a good job Bobs never heard her. That would have put the kibosh on Christmas.

We'd been going along lovely. Out round the craft markets, and stopping for steak and chips and mojo sauce about half twelve. He even got me out on a pedalo, Boxing Day afternoon. Then on the Friday he decided he was going to have a go at this jet-skiing, so I went up to the pool on the roof terrace for a bit of sun. I didn't realize it was one of them nude places, not till I got up there. Some of them was altogether in the altogether, brown as conkers, and all shapes. You didn't have to win no beauty contests to get your kit off up there. So I thought I might as well go topless, at any rate. I mean, topless is nothing these, days.

I don't know why I mentioned it. I should just have kept my mouth shut. He need never have known.

He said, 'What did you want to go and do that for?'

I said, 'Thought I'd try it. First time I'd ever tried

it. And why not? It's nice. Specially swimming.'

He said, 'First time and last time. I don't want blokes goggling at my wife's bazooms.'

I said, 'What about if I do it on the balcony?'

He said, 'Oh, yes, and have men with binoculars looking at you from that place opposite. Three-star place, full of scumbags.'

He can be that pig-headed when he wants to be. So we had words and I went down to the bar. I had two Ronmiel Sunsets and I got talking to a couple from Ipswich, got a curtain and blinds business and six grandsons. Next thing I know, in walks Bobs in that ivory rig with the flowers and sits down with us as cool as you like. And the funny thing was, nobody missed a beat. That's the English for you. Don't matter where you go in the world, nobody's got manners like the English, and I don't care what Diane's mum says about New Zealand.

Everybody just carried on talking, and we got another round of drinks. Even Ferdie the barman didn't let me down. Bobs ordered for everybody and Ferdie never batted an eyelid. I suppose they have to learn about things like that at hotel college. I suppose they have to learn how to deal with all sorts. He gave us time to drink up, and then he got one of the boys from the front desk to come and say we were wanted on the phone.

I never did find out what the manager said to him. I was just glad we were leaving first thing on Sunday. I got in the lift and went up without him, but he wasn't far behind, grinning like a blummin' loon.

I said, 'I don't think there's anything to smile about.'

He said, 'They didn't notice. That couple had a drink with me and they never noticed.'

I said, 'You're round the bend. Of course they noticed. Ferdie noticed.'

He said, 'That was because he's served me every night this week. But *they* didn't notice. Trust me, Ba. I'm getting a feel for these things.'

So that really got me worried. Messing around at home, that's one thing. I don't like it, but I can put up with it. But walking into the Helios Bar with his wig looking all wiggy and thinking he's passed off all right as my sister? That's really taking leave of your senses. The only thing I could hope was that they don't have anything like that in Ipswich, because one thing I do know is, most people see what they expect to see. The only thing I hope is that the both of them had bad eyes.

Melody was round in her lunch hour, first day back after the close-down. She said, 'Well, thanks for telling me you were going away. I had to phone Jason to find out where you were.'

I said, 'Happy New Year to you, too, Mel. And, yes, thank you, we had a nice time.'

She said, 'I was ringing you and ringing you on Boxing Day. We were moving furniture so we could decorate, only Andy's got a frozen spine. We could have done with a hand. I kept ringing and ringing. I thought you must be dead.'

I said, 'No, I was drinking Banana Smoothies and playing mini-golf with your father.'

She said, 'Does that mean everything's back to normal?'

I said, 'When was there ever anything normal about this family?'

She said, 'You know what I mean.'

I met Mary later on, to have a look round the sales. Fleur hadn't made it home for Christmas, of course. Pressure of work, Mary said.

I said, 'I hope you've learned your lesson. Kids don't want to be bothered with you once they've got lives of their own. You should have come with us. We had a smashing time.'

She said, 'Yeah. Well, next time, eh? You didn't have any problems then? With people at the hotel?'

I said, 'What do you mean, problems?'

She said, 'Well, we've got used to you with no hair. But I just thought other people . . . you know how people can say things, not thinking . . . I thought you might have a few sticky moments. And Bobs . . . you know . . . you must admit . . . How is Roxy, anyway?'

I've told that many people, I know it off by heart now. She's on tablets: one lot she has to have every day, and there's another kind she has to take once a week, and then there's an injection once a month. She'll have to keep going in for check-ups, of course, and she's got to stay on all this medicine for two years, but after that she should be in the clear. She'll even start getting her hair back in a bit, and then I can stop looking like a freak. I said, 'Come the summer I'll be able to meet you in Rackham's for a coffee without my head in a bag.'

Course, I might not. I might just keep it this way for the hot weather. Like Scouser always says, it grows on you, not having hair growing on you.

She said, 'It's not myself I mind for, Ba. It's you. People can't help staring.'

I said, 'It don't bother me any more, Mary.'

She said, 'And how's things with Bobs?'

I said, 'Oh, didn't I tell you? He had the sex change while we were away.'

We was buying towels and the lad's face that was parcelling them up was a picture.

I said, 'Yes. It's a lot cheaper out there. Couple of snips, a few stitches, and he was out shopping for leather skirts the next morning. And they done that little warty thing on the side of his nose. They chucked that in for free.'

She said, 'Ba! Keep your voice down. I didn't mean *that*. I meant, you know? Grounds for divorce?'

So I took her for a mochaccino and we had it all out, one last time, because I'll be jiggered if I'm going to explain it to her again. When I'd finished she said, 'Well, Ba, all I can say is, Bobs is a very lucky man. In fact, that's exactly what Douglas said, when you told us you were going away for Christmas. He said, "I hope Bradshaw realizes what a lucky man he is." I think you're very brave.'

I said, 'No. Too much of a coward to be on my

own. I just couldn't face starting all over.'

She said, 'Me neither. Even if I have just spent Christmas cooped up with old face-ache. Oh, it was a dreary Christmas, Ba. And New Year. All we done was watch telly. Why don't you come round tonight and we can have it again, like old times?'

So we bought smoked salmon, Marks's Chicken in Red Wine, and Chocolate Truffle Gateau to have at their place later on, and we phoned the lads to tell them to meet us at the clubhouse after work.

Bobs was held up. They'd, been called out to a big recovery job on the M40, two cars and an HGV, so it was all hands on deck, and he wanted to ride out with young Gary and make sure this new underlift gear is up to the mark.

Clive Astley was in the clubhouse when we got there, propping up the bar as per and bending the steward's ear, but nobody else was in. 'Oh,' he said, 'if it isn't the lovely mesdames Vickery and Bradshaw.' *Mesdames*.

He said, 'And how's that magnificent beast of yours? Still in good fettle, I trust. Still on a trajectory for Classic success?'

Mary smiled at him and said 'Yes', but I'm beggared if I knew what he was on about, so I'm blummin' sure she didn't. I ordered gin and tonics and asked Ken to bring them to us in the alcove down the far end. I didn't want to sit listening to Clive's silly twaddle.

Mary said, 'I've been thinking about this horse racing. You know how the jockey wears Bobs' colours? Well, shouldn't we have our own colours? You and me?'

I said, 'We could do.' I bet she wouldn't have been saying that if they was Scouser's colours.

She said, 'Cerise'd be nice. Cerise and sky blue.'

I said, 'You can't have any old colours, you know? There's set colours. And you can't have them if somebody else has got them.'

She said, 'Or, like a salmony pink and cream. Who's going to stop us?'

I said, 'Weatherby's. You have to register your colours, and you can't have any old thing. The Jockey Club won't allow it,' and then Scouser come rushing in, all of a flutter. He said, 'You'll never guess who I've just seen on the way in. Bev Bevan.'

Mary said, 'Is he a member?'

Scouser said, 'Looks like he might be joining. Wouldn't that be something? Meeting old Bev on the fairway?'

Bev Bevan was God to Scouser. We all liked them. We liked the whole band. I liked Carl Wayne. He was the singer. And Bobs wanted to be Trevor Burton. He used to pretend our frying pan was a guitar. But

Bev was Scouser's big hero, because drummers always act lary.

Mary said, 'We're getting our own racing colours. Me and Ba have decided on cream and salmon, so you'll have to phone the authorities tomorrow and tell them.'

He said, 'Yes, lover. Bev Bevan. I wonder what his handicap is?'

Mary said, 'We're waiting for Bobs. Why don't you ring his mobile, Ba? See if he's on his way.' So I did, but he weren't answering.

She said, 'I hope he's not going to turn up all oily.'

Bobs never turns up oily. To look at his hands you'd never guess what business he was in. He could be a brain surgeon, to look at his hands.

Scouser said, 'How's Roxy going on, and that little bab? Did she tell you? We were hanging around till Christmas Eve morning waiting to hear if Fleur was coming or not. I told her not to get her hopes up.'

Mary said, 'She couldn't help it, Douglas. She can't just drop everything.'

Scouser said, 'No, well. All I'm saying is we could have gone to Tenerife. How long is it since we seen her?'

Mary said, 'Keep your voice down.' But it didn't matter because there was still nobody in apart from Clive Astley, and he was three sheets to the wind.

Scouser said, 'Do you know, Ba, sometimes I think we shall never see her again.'

I said, 'What a way to talk. Why don't you and Mary clear off and visit her. Anybody'd think Seattle was the other side of the world.'

I could tell the minute I seen Bobs' face he was pleased with this new equipment. We've paid a lot out for it, but, like he said, you don't really know how good it is till you've got seven tons to bring in in a blizzard.

Scouser said, 'About time, too. My belly thinks my throat's cut.'

He's always hungry, Scouser. Always looking for your biscuit tin when he comes round.

Scouser fetched him a half, and he was going to get us another round but Mary said, 'We've got champagne in the fridge back at our place, haven't we, Ba? We're having New Year's Eve all over again.' He said, 'Suits me. Just let the workers have a nice cold beer and then we can be on the move. And speaking of The Move, Bradshaw, have I got news for you. Guess who I seen?'

He's like the boy that cried wolf, Scouser. He's claimed to see that many big names nobody believes a blind word he says any more.

We'd just got outside, and Mary was deciding whether to ride with me or Scouser. There was something in the air, more like sleet than snow, and the wind was raw. All I heard Scouser say was, 'Ain't it turned muggy?' and he was on the floor. There was sweat all along his top lip and he was rubbing his arm, rubbing it and rubbing it, like he had a cramp.

Bobs took one look at him and went running back inside. He shouted back to me, 'Keep him warm, Ba. Get my reefer out the car.'

Mary kept saying, 'He's come over faint. It's the sudden change. Out of that warm bar and into this cold wind.'

Bobs come back out, with Ken and Skinner, the club secretary. He said, 'There's an ambulance on the way. How's he doing?'

He'd stopped rubbing his arm, and he was just lying there, propped up against Mary. She said, 'He doesn't need an ambulance. We should get him off this wet ground. Could you walk inside, Douglas? If we give you a hand?' and he nodded.

Bobs said to leave him where he was, but Skinner and Ken were trying to get him up, and Clive Astley had come out, getting under everybody's feet. Then two men come down the steps and run across to help.

One of them said, 'Are you all right, mate? I felt a bit faint myself when I heard what it costs to join.' It was Bev Bevan.

Scouser's face was a picture. He said, 'Bev,' and then he was gone. Just like that.

Bobs was yelling at me to do mouth-to-mouth, but I didn't know what to do. He said, 'You must do, woman. All them hospital shows you watch.' He was just upset. Mary was the only one that was calm. She said, 'He's probably had nothing to eat since breakfast.'

Ken did have a go, him and Skinner, doing the breathing and pressing up and down on his heart, but we all knew really. Bev run down to the gate to show the ambulance where to pull in, and we kept looking at our watches and listening for the siren. But we knew.

Bobs said, 'I'll go with him. You follow with Mary.'

I thought she might argue, but she didn't. It hadn't sunk in.

She did say, 'Couldn't they go a bit faster?' because they were taking it steady. They had the blue light on, but I suppose they do that to make you feel they haven't gave up.

She said, 'Do you think it could be his heart? He's never had any trouble before. His dad never had any trouble with his heart.'

That's because the Johnny Walker got him first, but I didn't say that. I didn't say anything.

There was nowhere to park. I suppose they were busy. There was a lot of flu going round, and people falling on the ice. By the time I'd found a space and we'd walked back, they'd got him in and taken him somewhere, and there was no sign of Bobs. I gave the girl on the desk Scouser's particulars and then we must have sat there fifteen, twenty minutes. A nurse said they'd come and tell us as soon as there was any news. And then I seen Bobs coming with coffees in plastic cups, trying to carry three and slopping it all over. I caught his eye and he just gave me a little shake of his head.

He put the cups on the floor and squatted down opposite Mary. He said, 'They couldn't do anything, sweetheart. The doctor'll be out in a minute, but they couldn't do anything.'

She said, 'What about a bypass?'

They took her in to see him, and me and Bobs sat in this little room they keep for bad news. He said, 'It's only half-past eight, Ba. He was right as rain an hour ago.'

I said, 'Did he come round? Did he say anything?'

He said, 'Course not. He was finished out on the car park. They put a machine on him in the ambulance, but there was nothing doing. Not a flicker. We shall have to take her home with us.'

A nurse brought her back to us after a bit. She said she'd bring some tea, but Mary said, 'I don't want tea. I've just had coffee.' But she hadn't. None of us had touched a drop.

I said, 'Have you got Fleur's number with you?'

She said, 'I don't know.'

I said, 'What time would it be there?'

Bobs said, 'Don't make no difference what time it is. She's got to be told. We'll phone from home. You come back with us Mary, and we'll phone Fleur from our place.'

I drove, with Mary in the front with me and Bobs in the back. She kept saying, 'He was still warm, Ba. I think they've made a mistake.'

It was only the beginning of the afternoon in Seattle, so we couldn't get Fleur at home. Bobs was onto Directory Enquiries for ages, trying to get her work number, and I was sitting with Mary, trying to knock her out with Remy Martin. She never cried. None of us did. I felt like there was only one little bit of my brain working, and it just kept playing the same bit of film, over and over – sitting in the bar, talking and laughing, and then Scouser rubbing his arm and smiling at Bev Bevan.

Bobs said, 'She's on her way, Mary. She'll phone us as soon as she knows what plane she's on.'

We got her to bed about midnight. I was wide awake, but Bobs looked fit to drop. He said, 'All them things he used to reckon he'd got wrong with him. Like when he said a tarantula had bit him, remember, that afternoon we took Jason's kite up the Lickeys? And the time he thought he'd got kidney trouble, only he'd ate all that pickled beetroot. But he was never ill really. I never knowed him have a day off work.'

I said, 'I'm glad you're here.'

He said, 'And I'm glad you're here, Ba.'

I didn't half hold him tight.

Fleur was getting in about seven in the morning, so Bobs said he'd drive down and fetch her while I sat with Mary. She's not been safe to be left since the day after. For a start she kept talking as if it hadn't happened. We took her home and she was faffing around, putting washing in the machine and dusting. We didn't know what to do with her. I talked to her doctor and he said it was normal, and then, a blummin' parson turned up on the doorstep. I don't know where he'd sprung from because I've never knowed Scouser and Mary go to church, not since the day Fleur was christened, but anyway, there he stood with a face like a week of wet Mondays, so I had to ask him in. That was when something clicked with her. She was screaming, 'Duggie, where's my Duggie?' It was horrible to hear.

I held her tight. She said, 'Why did he go and leave me all on my own, Ba? He knows I'm no good on my own.' I was holding her and rocking her, but all the time I was watching Bobs over the top of her head, offering the parson the sugar bowl and trying to remember his etiquette. I was looking at him that hard, so I remembered every little thing about him, because Scouser hadn't been gone even a day and I couldn't remember his face, didn't matter how much I tried.

We took her back to the hospital that afternoon because she said she wanted to see him, and I went in with her while Bobs went for a little walk on his own. I felt a bit spare, standing there while she was saying goodbye to him, but I was glad I had been because she went to pieces and I near enough had to carry her out of there, and anyway, once I'd seen him, then I knowed it really was true.

After that the doctor put her on tranks, till she was over the worst, he said, and I just about moved in there. It was like living with a baby again, coaxing her to eat a drop of soup, up half the night with her sobbing. She'll never stay in that big house on her own. She'll never be safe to be left. She don't even know where her stopcock is.

It was just before twelve when Bobs got back with Fleur. She hadn't half put on some weight. That's America for you. We were in Florida once, and they never stop eating.

When she seen me she gave me a big smile and that started me off because she's the image of her dad. We all had beer and sandwiches. I said, 'We haven't made any arrangements. We thought you and your mum . . .'

She said, 'Sure. I only have a week.'

Bobs gave me a look. That's one thing about our pair. They may be useless, but at least they're only a few minutes' drive away.

I said, 'Will you want to go and see your dad?' They'd took him to the funeral parlour, and you could go and see him in the Chapel of Rest if you phoned up and asked them.

She said, 'I guess.'

When we were clearing away I said, 'Will Pete fly over for the funeral?'

She said, 'Who's Pete?'

It was a relief to get back to my own house. Bobs said, 'Do you think we've done the right thing? She's not much good with her mum, is she? They don't seem to have much to say.'

I said, 'And you realize there's no fiancé?'

He said, 'No fiancé, no weekend boat, no intention of ever coming back here.'

I said, 'What about Mary? How will she be fixed?'

He said, 'She should be all right. I don't know. Can't see her running the business, can you? Can't see her running anything. Anyway, I've told her, anything she needs, specially if she's a bit short till the will's sorted out, we'll tide her over. Right? If it had been the other way round, Scouser would have looked after you.'

He would. He'd have looked after me a bit too much.

He said, 'I'm sorry about this, Ba, but there's something I've got to do. I keep thinking "next week" and "when it's a better time", but there's no such thing as a better time, and then you run out of "next weeks", like Scouser did. You can't bank on "next weeks".'

I knew it. I've got that I can see the signs. Like when Roxy was really poorly. That's when he seems like he can't settle, can't relax until he's out of his trousers and into a skirt. Me, I'm just the opposite. I'm always in my shell suit round the house.

He said, 'I want to go out. I want to go out dressed and walk down the street. I've got to do it, Ba.'

We cremated Scouser on Thursday, and Mary went back to Seattle with Fleur on Saturday. It didn't affect me that much, the funeral. The parson kept talking about Douglas, and he was never Douglas to me. He was Duggie till we were about fourteen, and after that he was Scouser.

Bobs took it very bad, though. Specially when they played 'You'll Never Walk Alone'. Mel and Andrew came, and Jason, so there was more Bradshaws there than Vickerys, and Mary did look a poor thing. She looked like she could hardly walk.

Bobs rode back with Fleur and Mary in the limo, and I stopped behind to get the names off the wreaths. All them lovely flowers and you never know who's sent what. I'd said I'd do it so Mary'd know, later on, and I was glad I had because there was a little posy from Roxy and Blair that Jason had never mentioned, and some nice cut flowers from Bev Bevan. He'd signed the card and everything. We'd never have heard the end of that if Scouser had been there to see it.

Nobody went back to the house. I'd asked Fleur if she wanted a hand doing a bit of a spread but she didn't seem interested. I think it's all drive-in funerals now over there. I weren't bothered. Last thing I felt like was handing biscuits round to strangers. Standing round gassing about what a great bloke he'd been. There weren't anything anybody could tell us about Scouser. It was like the end of an era for us. That's how Bobs put it, and he was right.

When we got home he went and sat in that boys' room, where him and Scouser used to play pool, and he sobbed and sobbed. He'd told Fleur he'd go to the undertakers and get the ashes. Keep them till Mary gets back and decides what she wants to do with them. But I can see who's going to end up fetching them. He's never going to face bringing his best friend home in a plaggy bag. It's always women that have to do things like that.

Anyway he quietened down after a bit, and then I heard him in the shower.

When he come down he was in his tartan skirt and his two-tone loafers with the fringing, and he was wearing some new earrings: matt-gold, curled round like a ram's horn, really nice.

He said, 'I'm going into town. I'm going to the bank for Mary, to pay some cheques in, and then I'm going in Healey's for some tights and a cup of tea. Are you coming?'

I said I'd drive him. I did need a few odds and ends, so I said I'd drive him, and I might meet him in the Eatery, if I felt up to it. I'm not ever having him thinking that I'm coming round to the idea, because I'm not.

I'd just left him, and who should come out of the NatWest but Della Astley. She must have walked straight past him. She said, 'What a tragedy about Douglas Vickery. We'd have come to the funeral, only we've got the builders.'

I said, 'Oh, well, say no more.'

She said, 'Do you think Mary'll sell up?'

Della's always hankered after that house. They've got a nice enough place, the Astleys, but they do get a lot of traffic noise, and she's always wanted a bedroom with a balcony over the garden. She can be a very envious woman, Della.

I was on pins in case Bobs come out the bank and seen us, but there must have been a queue. I never thought I'd be pleased about a queue in a bank, but it saved my day. I didn't see him again till I got to the Eatery, and there he sat with a pot of tea and a plate of scones.

See, I don't know any more, because I keep seeing

him dressed up, I don't know how obvious it is. He might be getting better at his make-up, and he definitely did the right thing getting rid of the Farrah wig, but he is still a big man. He's got big hands. I know he's keen to get some rings, but I think his hands are too big for anything a woman might wear. I think he'd be better sticking to his wedding band, if he don't want people staring. But that's the thing I'm not sure about with Bobs. Sometimes I think he don't want anybody to notice, and then sometimes I think he's the biggest blummin' show-off I ever met. I mean, we didn't have to go to that Eatery.

He said, 'The scones aren't much cop. Dry as a nun's bazoom.'

I could have got us a nice cream cake to take home. Sitting there, wondering who might walk in. And they never give you enough butter.

I said, 'Well? How did you do?'

He said, 'Did Della say anything?'

I said, 'No. Did anybody else?'

He said, 'No. The girl in the bank looked at me, but it was probably because she's used to seeing Mary or Scouser. And the woman on Tights never even looked up. She was telling her friend about her car. I could have been the Elephant Man and she wouldn't have noticed. I was sweating though. I was sweating every minute of it.'

I said, 'Ladies don't sweat, Bobs. Horses sweat, men perspire, and ladies glow.'

He said, 'Is that right? Well let me tell you, this lady was glowing like an effing carthorse.'

Using a word like that in Healey's Eatery.

Melody's expecting. It's due the beginning of October. She's not very well at all, though. Morning sickness, only it lasts all day. I was just the same.

Bobs is over the moon, of course. He said, 'I've been thinking. We could build a playhouse.'

I said, 'You can get them from Argos and they pack away flat.'

He said, 'No. I mean *build* one. Like a proper little house. Roxy'd love it, and then, as the other babs get older . . . It'd be better than getting the swimming pool. Forever worrying one of them's going to wander off and get drownded. What do you think?'

I didn't want to say what I was really thinking. About how much we'll be seeing of any of them. Jason and Diane haven't been over here once since the nasty business. We're allowed to go there now, and we did take Roxy down to see Tiger Lil, but they never ask us to babysit, and I can see it'll be the same story with Mel. The Godbolds'll be in there staking their claim.

I said, 'Yeah. That'd be a nice thing to do on the weekends.' He needs something to do. Since Scouser. He's never been back to the golf club since that night. And he could do it. Bricklaying, plastering, anything like that. He's always been handy.

He said, 'I'll be the foreman, and you can be the navvy. That'll be a novelty.'

We had the Buttons and Bows crowd over. Bobs said it really was our turn. Peggy and Stephanie, Carole and Jill, Arlene and Michelle, Cynthia and Jenny. That Georgette didn't come, which was a good thing because I didn't like him one bit, and Vicky and Doris didn't come. Apparently Doris took an overdose, but she's going to be all right.

I done Black Velvets and bubble and squeak, as it was St Patrick's night, but then I was worried about some of them driving home. It's too easy to drink that stuff.

He was helping me clear away. He said, 'Do you know, Ba, I think I might call it a day with these meetings?'

I thought, Halleblumminlujah, he's cured.

But he said, 'There's one or two of them I wouldn't mind seeing. Just see them, like friends? But it's this club thing. Like we're all in a hole together? I don't think I'm cut out for clubs.'

Well we knew that already. That was why he left the Elks and he never really bothered with the Rotary.

He said, 'The thing is, I'm doing what I'm doing now, and everybody that needs to know knows, and we're over all the trouble.'

I gave him a long hard look when he said that.

He said, 'I know, I know. You've been brilliant, Ba. I know it's not been easy for you.'

I said, 'Still isn't. And don't you think for one minute I shall ever get used to it. Don't you kid yourself.'

He said, 'No. I know.'

I said, 'What do you think your mum would have said?'

He said, 'Oh, she knew.'

She never did. If she'd have knowed, I'd have knowed.

He said, 'She caught me in some of our Pat's stuff one afternoon, so she gave me a good hiding for going in her room.'

I said, 'And then what?'

He said, 'I told her I liked wearing dresses, so she gave me another good hiding for telling lies.'

You always knew where you stood with Bobs' mum.

The Dress Circle

We were just putting the lights out when the phone rang.

Jason said, 'You've got to come. She's in intensive care having fits.'

That journey took for ever. There was nothing on the roads but it felt like we were driving through treacle. Bobs said, 'Say your prayers, Ba,' and I didn't know which to pray for first, Roxy or not getting breathalysed. We run into that place and up the stairs, and a nurse said Jason was in a little sitting room. He was grey. He even let his dad put his arms round him.

He said, 'They think it's the measles.'

I said, 'Has she got a rash?'

He said, 'No. But they still think it's measles. It's because of her treatment. They catch things easy with this treatment, and they think it's gone to her brain. Measles can go to your brain.'

I said, 'Start at the beginning. Tell us what happened.'

He said, 'She was fine. Then she'd got a bit of a cough, hardly anything. I got home from work and she was playing with her Spirograph, nothing wrong. Then Diane bathed her, and I was just going to read her a story and she had like a fit. She was out for a few minutes, and when she come round she didn't know where she was.'

I said, 'And then what?'

He said, 'Diane phoned the ward, and Sister Galloway said dial 999 and keep her quiet in a dark room. So that's what we did. Next door took Blair, Diane came with her in the ambulance, and she had another fit just before they got here.'

We must have sat there an hour before anybody came to us. I've seen enough of hospitals to last me a lifetime this past twelve months. The doctor said she was stable but very poorly. He said we could go in, but only one at a time, and it might help to talk to her. He said she might be able to hear us.

Bobs said, 'How do you mean, might be able to hear us?'

The doctor said, 'She's in a coma. We can't be sure what she's aware of.'

I don't know what day of the week it is. We've been taking turns to sit with her, and taking turns to have Blair. Even Mel's took a turn, so wonders'll never cease. We've been playing her favourite tapes, and Bobs has been talking the hind leg off a donkey, telling her about this playhouse he's planning and threatening to run off with her Smarties if she don't hurry up and open her eyes.

She's been twitching a little bit. Diane thought she felt her squeeze her hand, and they say that's a very good sign, but they're worried about her breathing, with her lying there all that time. They're worried about her getting pneumonia.

Mack's running Tiger Lil at Thirsk, but we shan't be going. Mary's not back and we're needed here. He said, 'She looks well enough, but fillies can be backward after the winter. I'd like her to have a run, as long as the ground's not too hard. Then we'll decide about the Guineas.'

Monday afternoon, Bobs was going to sit with her while Diane had a rest, and I was just looking in on her when she opened her eyes. She said, 'Where's my grandad?'

Course, they let him in, as soon as the doctor had had a look at her.

He said, 'About time, too, young lady. Do you know how long I've been sat here talking to this wall?'

She said, 'I could hear you, Grandad. And my mum and my dad and Nana Ba. I could hear you. But I was busy talking to Uncle Scouser.'

He said, 'Oh, yeah? And what did he have to say?'

She said, 'He told me to get better and give Tiger Lil a big kiss.'

Bobs looked at Diane and Diane looked at me, and I felt all the little hairs that I haven't got stand up on the back of my neck.

So Mack took Tiger Lil up to Thirsk and ran her over a mile. She was second to Moonsaballoon in the Rossi Plant Hire Stakes, but the ground was harder than she likes it, so he's not downhearted. She goes in the Guineas.

Bobs was dancing round in his fluffy slippers,

singing 'Here we go, here we go, here we go,' and then he phoned Mary in Seattle. He said, 'Get back here woman. Scouser's turning in his urn.'

You should have seen the convoy. Me and Bobs up front with Mary and Roxy. Then Jason and Diane with Blair, Mel and Andrew, and even the Godbolds. I'd made Mary come out with me and get a new outfit. She's not been bothering with herself while she's been staying at Fleur's. She said it rains all the time in Seattle and you just feel like shooting yourself.

Anyway, we got her a really nice blue swing-back coat and a red-and-blue hat.

She said, 'You don't think it's too bright, do you? Under the circumstances?'

I said, 'Blummin' heck, Mary, Scouser wouldn't want you dressing like some old Italian widow woman.'

I got a jacquard two-piece, duck-egg blue and gold, and some big turquoise earrings, and we bought Roxy a pair of patent shoes to go with her new coat and hat. Not that she ever wears the hat. It don't bother her any more, people seeing her noddle box. It don't bother me neither. Although, as Mary said, it can blow chill at Newmarket.

The telly people were there, of course, it being a big race, and Brough Scott interviewed Mack. She was 15/1 overnight with Ladbroke's and the *Racing Post* said she was one to watch. By the time we got to the course her price had come in to 10/1, and I couldn't eat a thing my guts were in such a flutter. There were nine runners. Lincoln Green and Spiffing Tuck were joint favourites. Spiffing Tuck had won the Craven Stakes, and Lincoln Green had beat Leylat Jameel at Newbury, but Bobs said, 'So what?'

Then there was Contarini, but she was just the pace-setter for the French lot, and Great Orme. All the papers said they were out of their class. So the only other ones we had to worry about was Tant-Pis-Pour-Toi, but I couldn't see a frog horse beating our girl; Designer Label, and some people were saying she was the danger because she'd beaten Moonsaballoon over a mile at York, but Mack said that result flattered her; and Vanessa Dear, the Irish grey. Oh, and Leylat Jameel. So them men in the shiny suits were back.

It was the jockey that was worrying me. Des Fogarty was injured, so we'd got Cronin Magee. Bobs said she couldn't be in a safer pair of hands, but I had a feeling she wouldn't like it, having a stranger on her back, and Mary agreed with me. Men don't understand these things.

She looked a picture in the paddock. Her stable lad won the prize for Best Turned Out, and Roxy thought that was it. She thought that was all we'd gone for. Blair had filled his nappy and I was worried Diane would miss the race, but Audrey Godbold offered to go and change him. She is a nice woman. I'd love my Antoine to have a go with her hair.

Tiger Lil went round from the paddock to the course as nice as you like, and then as soon as she seen the rails she stopped, and she didn't get moving again until every other horse had gone past her. Bobs was sweating. Melody was cussing. Anyway, then she went sideways. She done three furlongs like a crab, and then she seemed to remember where she was, and she went down to that start and into the gate like a little angel. She went off at 3/1.

Contarini went straight up front, so the papers were right about her, and the rest of them were bunched that tight you couldn't make out who was doing what. Bobs and Andrew and John Godbold were watching through their glasses, and Melody kept saying, 'Let me have a turn. Let me see.'

They split, about four furlongs out. Designer Label

had got herself boxed on the rails with Tant-Pis-Pour-Toi, Lincoln Green and Vanessa Dear, so that's getting to be a bit of a habit with her, and then Tiger Lil was running nice and free with Spiffing Tuck, Leylat Jameel and Great Orme. Contarini was finished, and Great Orme was dropping back. Then Spiffing Tuck and Leylat Jameel started to make headway, and the grey was still in it, but Tiger Lil was losing touch, and there was Designer Label to worry about, as well, just nudging her way through, getting out of trouble.

I couldn't watch. I'd got Roxy sitting on my hip, weighing a ton for somebody who was at death's door a few weeks ago, so I just put my face against her collar and closed my eyes. I heard Bobs. 'That's it, Magee,' he said. 'That'll do nicely.' Then I heard John Godbold say, 'She'll do it. She's going to do it,' and then the whole blummin' stand was roaring. I've never heard nothing like it. I opened my eyes and she was blasting past Leylat Jameel. Designer Label was making ground, but then there was a bit of a bump between her and Vanessa Dear, and that left our baby battling it out with Spiffing Tuck, all the way to the line, and she took it by a neck.

If Scouser hadn't have had his coronary when he did, he'd have had one then. Bobs picked Mary off her feet, and Andrew was red as a lobster, trying to shake his hand. Blair was chortling, and Roxy was jumping up and down like she was on a spring, and even our Mel come and give me a big wet kiss. I felt like I'd run that race myself.

We all pushed down to the paddock to cheer her in, and I'll swear she knew. Bobs always says horses were in the queue for legs and teeth when the brains were being dished out, but I think they know when they've won. I said to Mary, '*Now*, are you glad I made you get a new rig?' She laughed, and I don't know that I could have done if I'd been in her shoes. I'd have gave anything to see Scouser's silly face in that Winner's Enclosure.

They called a stewards' inquiry, but Bobs said, 'Nothing to do with us. Designer Label banged into the grey, but it won't affect us.'

Everybody was shouting and shoving, trying to get up close. Mack nearly lost his hat. Me and Mary went up together to get the trophy, and everything was in a mist. Then Derek Thompson wanted to talk to us for Channel 4, but Mary lost her tongue, and so did I for a minute. I'd got Roxy pulling on my arm, wanting to go and see Tiger Lil get washed down, and Mack whispering he'd got a runner in the next race and he was needed in the weighing room.

Bobs was burbling like a loon about how he'd always had every confidence in her, and how we was starting a fund with the winnings, the Scouser Vickery

Memorial Fund, for kiddies with leukaemia. First I'd heard. Then Derek Thompson said, 'And Barbara, two members of the family with the same hair cut? I believe there's a bit of a story?'

I said, 'Well, it's Roxanne here . . .' I didn't know what to say. I'd just won the 1000 Guineas, and he was asking me on live telly about where my hair had gone.

Bobs said, 'It was when Roxy was in hospital, weren't it, sweetheart? Roxy's hair fell out, so Ba thought, Right. She's always been a slave to fashion, that woman.'

Thommo laughed. He said to Roxy, 'And what do you think about it?'

Roxy said, 'I think it's nice. And my grandad sometimes wears dresses.'

Bobs jumped right in. He said, 'I dunno, Derek. You put that little cross in the box for no publicity, and what happens?'

And then they called the outcome of the stewards' inquiry, which was just as well because there was no sign of that hole in the ground opening up and swallowing me.

When it was all over, I took Mary to one side. I said, 'I'm sorry. I never knowed that was going to come out. I really, really didn't know.' When Mary's in a mood she's got a face that'd stop a tank. She said,

'It's not you, Ba. It's him. Forty-five years and he still can't get it right. Forty-five years and he has to go on the telly and say that Scouser business.'

I said, 'I'm sorry.'

She said, 'I'm just relieved Douglas wasn't here to hear it,' and all them little neck hairs I haven't got stood on end again.